THE CAPTAIN
OF THE CREW

By Jackson Rezen

TRICHOTOMY MEDIA

The Captain of The Crew
By Jackson Rezen
Copyright ©2022 by Jackson Rezen.

First printing 2022
Trichotomy Media
captainofthecrew.com

DEAR READER

YO! Thanks for checking out my book. Whether you are a family member or friend who feels socially obligated to buy, or you are simply a wonderful person who genuinely has interest enough to pass the main blurb, I think you will truly enjoy this story. Writing it has mostly become a way for me to dump my existential dread into the world but, as it turns out, it's really just a banger. Though it is primarily a character driven story, there is enough action to knock your socks off and a few cool tech things that I thought sounded nifty, plus some good comedy. Oh, and death and stuff, too. The main characters all have letter monikers which is a little Tarantino-y but, I was in film school when I came up with the concept. Sue me.

If you enjoy the story, or at least shed a single tear, please let me know. One day, when I die, I'd like to know I left something worth reading behind.

I'm just kidding. I'm gonna live forever. You can put it on the stone.

– Jackson

TABLE OF CONTENTS

F160

EXO
SHELL

120"

h8'0"

HYDROLICS
MOTOR BOIS?

3' SIDE
CLEARANCE

ED 471
59 83

90
TIME

???WED
ED.
WELD EQUIP

FILED - REFURB SIMPSON TRUCKS
- BACK / TIRES
CALL MIKE

* ROOF RACKS PEDS / CUSTOM ??
* GET BREAKAWAY MAGNETS FOR REACTION
* BUMPER GUIDES ~24"

ACME CORP PARK LEASING
18 MOS. OCT // 9 AM MARCIA
837 - 1159 - x: 3:25

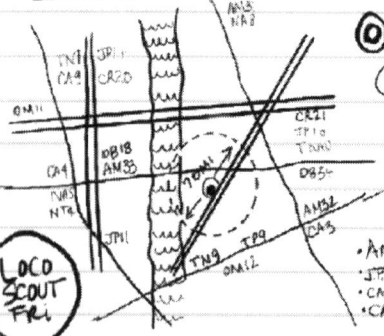

LOCO
SCOUT
FRI

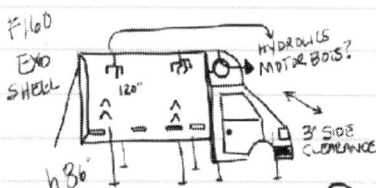

01 SECURE SPACE
02 SECURE TARGET
03 TECH SET
04 SECURE PII / PIN
05 TRANSPOR
06 OUT

OSLO?

charlie

Dr. Bowman
Ped RT 4/13
3.5 / 7
O₂ / Bx least - Thur
RR Supplies

$

3+ Avg x 15
37 M BY MAR.
SPLITS
35/30/20/15
C T D G

FISHES
WISHES

SAM
SN CHECK

9AM

· AM BANK   · TRUE HOST +
· J.P. S'BANK   · NATIONAL TRUST
· CARNEGIE   · OMNI BANK
· CAPITAL   · ONE MONEY

CWC

SAM(T)ECH 897-894

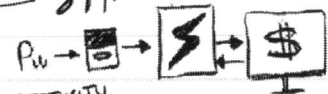

TECH | POWER COMP BANK | $ $P_W \rightarrow$  $\rightarrow$ ⚡ $\rightarrow$ $

?? • CONNECTIVITY
• BLOOD SOURCE
• POWER BW

• SOFTWARE
• COMPATIBLE?
• HARD DRIVE TRANSFER

• FW BYPASS
• LOGIN/PW

||||| |||

GESTURE TRAX
Shelly NW Hosp.

ED CONTACT ♥ BOT
★ ___

78BPM STORAGE
BUILT PADS
CDT

↓ Kel

| IV BUS - SET PORTS |

DOC

4 MIN

MED BAG:
- FENT/KET ×2
- CAUTERIZER
- GAUZE/ALCOHOL
- SYRINGES
- ?? CALL DOC ⟶ ●

B.J. 4 FENT/KET ★★
489-5162 $400
After 6pm

PSYCHLOCKS
⑨ CALL HOSP SEC
895-6531
x# 4311

SAM 10 GARAGE
TUES
• characters
• game plan
• guard trxn

↓

NYSEQ !!!!   32#
231
-6

ADVANTAGE TRUCK
GRAPHICS FOR
SCHEMATICS - Ed
WWW.ADGRAPHIX.COM
Login: CWC
PW: 4Charlie
★

THE CAPTAIN
OF THE CREW

PROLOGUE

Sparks flew up and disappeared into the air, a cloud of rapidly expanding fireballs exploding and vanishing. Some made it to the ground and danced or bounced away before running out of sustenance. The sound of hissing air and crackles filled the space. The torch was extinguished, and the clicking of a socket wrench took its place. Metal dragged and fire burned. Hard rock played loudly on the speakers, drowning out the ambient clangs as the two men moved around each other. The floor was scattered with tools and carts. One of the men ducked out to a small office next to the mechanic's bay.

Ed set his welder down and pulled his mask off. His black hair stuck to his forehead and hung loosely over his neck. He pushed it back and tucked a small piece behind his ear, the sweat holding it in place. In front of him sat the large frame of a box truck without wheels, propped up on jack stands. He picked up a remote and pressed a button. The back door of the truck swung out and up like an old garage, revealing an empty space on the inside. Where the truck bed and axles should have been was only the concrete of the shop floor. Four walls and, in the front, the exoskeleton of a truck cab. There was nothing but air from the rear door straight through to the windshield. Ed hung his welding torch on a hook and took a quick lap around the monstrosity. It was weeks' worth of work, day in and day out—all the mechanics, the welding, the detailing. From the outside, it was a boring white box truck, but what it meant was limitless.

"Hey, C," he called across to the office. "I think that's it."

"Ready to test it?" C returned to the garage from the office with two cans of beer, set one down, and cracked the other. The smell of sweat and burnt ozone clung to everything, but it made the beer taste better. He grabbed a key ring and walked out to the parking lot.

* * *

The night air was crisper than C was expecting and he let out a light shiver with the breeze. The lights from the signs on the other commercial units in the complex lit the asphalt but otherwise, the night was dark and quiet. The haunting silence of an industrial park in the late hours of the night was uncanny and surreal. There was a subtle drone of a small highway a mile west; cars passed every twenty seconds or so, breaking the illusion of solitude. In those twenty seconds, if life vanished from Earth, there would be no record, no complaint. The mind can edge on the thought, revel in the curiosity; the romance of freedom. There, in those silent moments, there was true freedom.

Three hours earlier, a mother, a father, and their son started their drive home from a vacation to the beach, and just now, their car rumbled loudly down the highway, pulling C from his reverie.

His breath stuttered, though it was hard to tell whether it was from the cold or the excitement. Things were moving. The van stood out from the darkness with a mild glow of the white siding. He walked quickly to it, popped the modified side view mirror out of its socket on the passenger side and moved around the back of the van. Once he was within a few feet of the driver's side door, the lights switched on and the door swung open gently, autonomously. He pulled himself in, the door closing itself behind him. By default, the seatbelt telescoped forward over his shoulder and then canted and snaked its way across his chest where it clicked itself in on the far side of his lap. C placed his foot on the brake and the vehicle started up. He lowered the driver's side window, dismounted the other rear view mirror and tossed it onto the passenger seat.

The large garage door of the shop opened as the van approached slowly. "Bring it to the right just a bit," Ed called, standing next to the truck shell. The van crawled its way into the frame. There was a faint skidding sound as the rubber bumpers slid along its sides. The van fit like a glove within the shell of the box truck, the van's cab resting exactly in the empty cab of the truck. There was a metallic clunk as the van's bumper met the inner bottom of the truck cab's grill plate. C took a deep breath.

"Alright, moment of truth." Ed hit another button on the remote. Metal claws along the ceiling of the truck's cargo compartment sprung into action, banging and ringing as they closed over the van's modified roof rack. There was a faint electric whirring that was followed by a clang and a much louder whirring as the structure shifted its weight to the top of the van and off the jacks. From the outside, the truck body lifted slightly and the stands rotated up and tucked themselves under the frame. The driver's side window lined up with the outside as the machine matched the height of the van. Finally, everything stopped. Braces in the truck's ceiling fell into place to take work off the hydraulics and to keep the truck cover from sliding. The windshields sat an inch from each other, nested like Russian dolls.

Ed's smile took over his face. He took a deep sigh of relief and started laughing. C crawled out the back of the van and matched his excitement. He stared at their creation for a minute, taking in the weight of the achievement. The possibilities grew closer. The checklist tallying off in his head. Ed lit a cigarette and exhaled slowly.

"Good job, man." C gave Ed a hard pat on the back. Ed's satisfaction melted away slowly.

"Thanks." His tone had diminished. "Hey, I gotta talk to you about something." Ed turned around and leaned his forearms on the table. C followed.

"Yeah? What's up?"

"I gotta back out."

C's face dropped. "Wait, what?"

Ed sighed. "I can't go, man. It's time for me to head out."

C stood up. "No... no, no, no. Ed, there is no plan without you."

"It's not a choice, man. I know the timing is bad but I don't make the rules."

"What is it this time?"

"It's a bit of a story. One of the parts got damaged by one of the movers and the guy is accusing me of hustling him."

"You talked to him?"

"Yeah, but you know the type. They're right. Doesn't matter what the reality is."

C rubbed at his face. "Fuck, man."

"Yeah. Shame they don't have a Better Business Bureau

The Captain of The Crew

for back alley dealings." He took another drag of his cigarette.

C paced away from the table. The gears in his head spun wildly. Two years in the making would come crashing down. All the time and money to get to this point would be for nothing. Ed broke the silence.

"I know a guy that can take over. He's a little out there but I think he's exactly what you need for crowd control. I'll send him your way."

C shook his head. "I don't know, man. I can't take risks like that. I'm already putting a lot of trust in this kid for the surgery. The guy with the gun can't be someone I don't know. Sam is gonna lose it."

"It'll be alright. He's from another crew. They got a little jostled and lost some people so he straightened out."

The two of them sat in silence for a while. C stared at Ed and shook his head. He was speechless. This man in front of him held the last tile of his thousand-piece jigsaw puzzle and he was taking it away to be replaced by what could only be a badly-cut replica. Time and time again they did this dance. Each time getting longer than the last. For all C knew, this could be the last time.

"Can you at least let me know where you're going this time?"

Ed chuckled lightly. "I'm not sure yet. Just can't be here."

"Fuck man. Won't be the same without you."

"You've managed before."

C took a deep breath. "When are you out?"

Ed smiled lightly. "Now, actually. I wanted to see this project through."

C nodded slowly, his lips tight.

Ed drummed his hands quickly on the table. "I won't

7

leave you with this mess though." They packed up the tools and Ed slung his bag over his shoulder. He grabbed a piece of scrap paper and scribbled something down.

"Here." He handed it over. "I don't know where I'll be, but if you need a place to get out to, you know, if El doesn't work out, hit me up."

C looked down at the numbers on the paper. "New number?"

"Had to leave some stuff behind."

C smiled. "Okay, man." A beat. "By the way, don't tell that new guy my name. C is enough."

"Sure, bud."

"Thanks." He put a hand out and Ed pulled him in for a hug.

With another pat on the back, he was at the door. "Hey," he stopped as his hand hit the handle. "My kid is still living in town. If you see him around, give him my best."

C nodded. "Will do."

1 | JAMES BILLMEN, THE HERO

The ceiling curved upwards, the walls running away from the ground with twisting columns, colliding at an apex—an explosion of paint and plaster. If someone were to stand in the center of the room and follow the wall up with their eyes, they would most certainly fall over backward by the time they got to the top. Twelve feet off the ground, a gold line raced around the room as the sun, refracted from the high windows, gleamed and sparkled. The building was an architectural masterpiece. Long ago, teams of men planned and drew, cut and carved, filed and drilled. They worked their hand tools, and dug the foundation with shovels and pickaxes, naive to the day a metal giant could scoop out all their days' work in an hour.

When it was first built, its only visitors indulged in the finer things, and wouldn't dream of hiding their money and jewels in a box behind the Christmas decorations. Instead, a bank was commissioned to house the fortunes of these aristocrats in steel rooms with steel doors surrounded by cement walls. It stood as a testament to riches and well-being, to the victory of wars, and the secret romanticism of will writing. Little did they know that, so many years later, the homeless would spend their nights outside, curled up in the spaces between the pillars, and the counter would be run by a duplicitously starry-eyed college graduate who told her old high school rivals that she had a successful career in "banking."

This was the fate of the True North National Bank, and while the streets outside had degraded a bit, the luxury of the branch was not lost. (And the security guards did their darndest to chase off the homeless.) The customers that filled the room wore expensive suits and designer skirts. Telephones rang and the plastic clicked as they were answered. "True North, how can I help you?" swam around the air. A twenty-foot TV stretched across the wall. A slide show of ways to "Invest the Best with True North" and "Secure your True Identity" flashed on the screen. They were never too busy, always a counter open, but that was to be expected with the requisite account balances and the annual minimums required on some of the offered credit cards which were brilliantly displayed in a glass box above the station that once held withdrawal and deposit forms. The cards even had their own spotlight. Unfortunately, they had become relics since the PII took over.

The center of the room was taken up by a long granite table. It was a bit too modern for the architecture, but so was most everything below the golden line which stood fast, like the KT boundary, protecting the old from the throes of the new. The far wall was split just below the line, seamlessly merging from the old gritty cement to smooth, crystal clear glass that fell to the floor. There were five stalls cut out for the tellers, who stood behind a grand wooden desk that ran, wall to wall, behind the glass. Four of the stalls were retro-filled by large screens. They looked hilariously out of place in the old cathedral style building. Shiny and silver, moving pictures on the screens and alien beeps and whirs. Modern banking for the modern world.

The last counter was occupied by a nicely-dressed girl. Tan skin, blonde hair, and sparkling blue eyes with a plastic-looking face that said, "I studied finance in hopes of breaking the mold and now I'm stuck in glorified customer service, but I'm going to make the best of it because I have to pay rent."

The bank was nearly empty. Two people tapped around on the fancy machines, and one spoke to the girl at the counter. A professionally overzealous banker in an office cubicle off to the side of the main room excitedly laid out the credit cards to an uninterested man and his cautious wife, as if to sell them on the aesthetic of the cards themselves, never mind the 28% interest and the $2,000 annual fee. "Feel the weight of this one." It was a vain attempt as the PII in each of their wrists could do all the same things, could not be lost or stolen, and they had really just come to the bank to merge their accounts.

An armed security guard stood watch near the door. He drank a coffee and rested his arm on the tire around his waist. If anything went down, he could dial 911 faster than anyone on this side of the Mississippi. The gun on his hip was loaded. When he bought the weapon, many years ago, he put fifteen rounds in the clip, popped it in the well, and there they sat till this day.

James Billmen walked in the door. A wireless earbud jammed in the side of his head, into which he was badgering a business partner who had "missed the point." His voice rose and fell, trying to assert dominance and then quickly realizing that he was in public. He did this in a measurable pattern. James stormed up to an open automated teller, slid his right wrist, palm down, under the scanner and waited for the confirming beep. He tapped

11

his thumb and middle finger together twice, rapidly, and, with the flick of the wrist, swiped his hand to the right. The screen spun out a series of images, "Welcome back, James," faded in on the top and a list of options dropped down in sequence. He punched at the touch screen, often a second or two quicker than the visuals could appear. It was half-hearted and he was obviously more preoccupied with expressing his unrelenting tirade on the concept of work ethic to the poor person on the other side of the phone.

The screen James was jabbing at suddenly went dark. A quick flicker of light and the sound of a mechanical sigh and then, there was nothing. His fingers lifted, as if putting up his hands in defense, in case the machine tried to punch him. He had had enough. As with most things in his life, when something went wrong, the best fix was to give it a good slap and blame someone else. He smacked the side of the machine in hasty anger which was apparently the wrong thing to do. The lights in the bank turned off. The other machines flashed white before going dark, and, like an orchestra warming up, there was a synchronous hum that came to a sudden metallic clank followed by silence. James looked around, hoping no one saw his temper tantrum which seemed to have broken the bank. He hung up his phone.

* * *

The customers all looked up at the now snuffed lights. Wondering if this was citywide or if this multibillion dollar corporation just couldn't swing the electric bill. The nicely-dressed girl at the counter reached for the phone, remembered that it too required electricity, and promptly walked away from the desk to find someone in charge. There were murmurs among the small crowd. A well-to-do businessman with a black computer case checked his watch, a large gold band holding a black and gold face. It might as well have had a hundred dollar bill pop out on the hour. He looked like he was on his way to a meeting and this whole situation was about to become terribly inconvenient. His watch read 12:02. The girl at the counter returned to assure the confused gaggle of patrons that everything would be just fine and that someone was looking into it.

The front doors swung open. Four men walked in, two carried small bags. They were dressed in jeans and skintight long sleeve shirts of different colors. There were no graphics or logos, plain shirts, plain pants, plain bags. All four men wore blue surgical masks, black beanies, and each had a headlamp, whose light glared over their faces. They walked in with a confidence, chest out, back straight. Their feet and movements were quick and deliberate. There was a theater to it, the way they looked around, the way they slung their bags to the side, the way they approached the man with the black computer case.

The girl at the counter reached below the desk and hit a button. The button. The "oh shit" button. As stated in the training video, "There will be a silent but firm click and the button will light up red to signal the police have been alerted." She pressed in and felt the click. She looked down, the light was not on. Of course the light was not on, there was no power. *Were the police called? Is it just the light that's out or is the whole system down? I was never trained for this.*

Then a lot of things happened all at once.

13

* * *

"ALRIGHT, MOTHERFUCKERS! WE'RE GOING TO MAKE THIS REEEAL QUICK!" The bright light from the man's headlamp masked his face. The silencer on the end of his gun was pointed at the head of the security guard who had one hand in the air and the other on his weapon. His coffee was on the ground.

"Both hands up."

The security guard complied, taking his hand off his weapon and holding it up in the air. The man with the gun reached to the guard's side and lifted the pistol from its holster, keeping his eyes on the patrons. "EVERYONE! BACKS TO ME, FACE TO THE WALL, HANDS OUT." He smashed the butt of the gun on the wall of a cubicle rapidly.

One of the crew with a bag sprinted towards the counter and vaulted over it, through the teller window, sticking the landing. The light from his headlamp bounced and refracted off the glass.

"Pardon me, ma'am. I'm going to need you to go on, take a seat on over there, on the ground, and not move a whole lot. We're not taking nothing from you so don't you worry." He was polite and spoke quickly. He had a southern drawl that was almost good enough to believe but it hit the clichés like a truck and he chuckled as he did it. She squinted as the glare from his headlamp blinded her.

The man with the gun made it to the counter. "Lady, what's the code?" He gestured to the keypad-locked door that led to the back offices.

The lady stared at him blankly.

"I know there are two people back there. What's the

code!?" He swung the barrel of his gun into a vase, sending glass and water flying across the room and shattering on the floor, narrowly missing a customer.

Another member of the four-man-crew's eyes darted up and gave him a hard stare.

The girl choked out a response. "9372."

The gunman walked to the door, punched in the code, and proceeded to sprint from office to office punching codes and pulling employees out to the front room.

* * *

The final two of the four men charged the man with the black computer case. He dropped his bag and put his arms up, pleading for what he assumed was his life. The men were holding two pieces of sheet metal, about five feet long and a foot wide. They were straight and rigid with a slight bend that ran down the center and rounded at the ends. One side had a thin layer of foam rubber that was cracked and worn. The man on the right held one of the metal pieces from the end, wound up, and swung it like a bat. He aimed low and slapped the sheet across the man's legs just above the knee. With an explosive crack, the sheet metal snapped and curled around itself like a broken spring—a giant metal snap bracelet with impressive force and strength. It wrapped around the man's legs, tightening and settling as he wiggled around. He reached down in pain, and now in position, was hit with the second sheet around his stomach just above his waist, arms and all. He was powerless, the metal turning him into a very well-dressed inchworm.

With a heave-ho, he was lifted and slung on the large

granite table in the middle of the room like a slab of beef in a slaughterhouse. He might as well have been a piece of meat, his body bound and his mouth stuffed with something that tasted like laundry detergent. He was a smart man, and quick to realize that he wasn't going anywhere.

The two men who had tied him down rummaged through a bag and pulled out small cases and gadgets. They were both tall, over six feet. It was hard to see past the shine of the headlamps, but when their heads were turned slightly the businessman could make out small features. One crewman had bright blue eyes. They were kind and calm and the blue contrasted well with the black of his beanie. A heavy brow rested over them, capable of giving intense expression, though none was showing now. He was well built, strong arms and broad shoulders. The skin on his wrists looked weathered, bathed in a light layer of black hair and ending in a pair of tight, gray surgical gloves. The other man was thinner and had dark skin. His brown eyes moved a little more frantically as he seemed to be focusing intently on what he was doing. He was younger too, maybe in his mid twenties. His hands moved deftly in the gray gloves, opening a roll of fabric and laying it out, presenting a small selection of shiny tools that glowed in the beam of light. There was a noticeable bump under both of their left sleeves on their forearms—like an armband they were wearing under the shirt but with a smaller bump sticking out of the bottom of it.

The businessman looked between them desperately. He tried to scream but the man who stood over him placed a large hand over his mouth and quietly told him to not do that or bad things would happen. The blue-eyed man wrapped a bulky black band around the businessman's forearm. A blue light flashed on it.

"What's your name?"

"Mm…Michael."

"Michael, I need your PIN."

The man shook his head in refusal.

"I really would rather do this the easy way but I can call G over here. He has a gun, and he likes the hard way."

Michael closed his eyes and moved his hand. He swiped his thumb along all four fingertips and then clenched his fingers down while keeping an open palm and released them quickly. A small orange light in his inner wrist quickly flashed green and then returned to orange. The blue-eyed man unclasped the band and ran to the counter.

* * *

"I told you to stay on the ground, you fat fuck!" The security guard had sat up and G wasn't happy about it. "What? They didn't teach you to lay down at obedience school? Only sit and eat? Well, you got one of those down didn't ya, ya fuckin' meatball." The guard grunted as he tried to lay back down but the hard tile was hurting his back.

"I said get down!" G put his heel into the guard's side. He groaned in pain. "Ha! It jiggles!"

The blue-eyed man gave him another look from across the room. G frowned and looked away. He had cleared the security guard's weapon, tossed it behind a desk, and started pacing the floor. He looked outside, surveying the area. Business carried on as normal and the "Closed" sign, which he had slapped on the door on their way in, was doing its job. He shifted his attention to the room. Over in the corner, near the first of the teller machine windows,

James Billmen stirred in his spot.

* * *

The masked man who had jumped behind the counter had unloaded a series of wires and a small cubed battery, with a couple of Edison plugs on one end. He got below the desk, unplugged the computer, and ran an extension cord to the cube which was also plugged into a USB slot on the computer. The monitor powered on, login screen ready.

"Ma'am, I'm going to need you to hop on up and log in for me." The girl did as she was told. *The bank is insured for this kind of thing, right? This was in the training, right?* The computer was sitting on the home screen. The man opened the banking software which again the girl logged into. The blue-eyed man handed him the band with the flashing blue light, which he also plugged into the cube and started typing away with gray gloved hands.

"How's he holdin' up?" The man at the computer did not look up and had dropped his accent.

"He's alright. Doc's about to knock him out." The blue-eyed man started to walk away.

"C," called the man at the computer. The blue-eyed man turned around and tilted his head up to redirect his headlamp.

"Give him a kiss goodnight for me." He took the time to look him in the eyes. C smiled and walked away. He looked at his watch.

"Two minutes," he yelled. The team echoed it back.

* * *

James Billmen was tucked up against a wall, a statue,

frozen in time, twitching his eyes back and forth. He was staring at G through the reflection on the metal floor lining of a cubicle. G turned his head away, looking out the front door. James slid his hand into his pocket, pulled out his phone, and set it between him and the wall. He returned to his position. Frozen. This was the game. Look away, move. Look back, freeze. The most cautious game of red-light/green-light ever played. Finally, he took a chance. He dialed 911 and set it on his lap. The phone slid off his thigh and bounced to his side sliding a little too far out away from his body for comfort. He reached to pull it back.

In the most unfortunate chain of events, as James reached for the phone, his finger drifted across the screen, and ever-so-gently accidentally pressed a little too hard on the speakerphone button.

"911, what's your emergency," rang out into the room: the voice of a young woman sent by the gods of the phone service to assist in any matter under the sun; a hero in the right place at the right time. This was the wrong place at the wrong time. G stormed towards him, gun pointed.

"What in the fuck do you think you're doing?"

The cards were on the table. There was no turning back now, and James was going to be the hero this time.

"The Cut Wrist Crew is at True North!" he cried out into the phone.

Now, maybe G was aiming for the phone, or the wall, or maybe he didn't even mean to pull the trigger, or maybe he knew exactly what he was doing. Either way, a bullet found its way out of G's gun, and in a flash at 12:04, James Billmen was dead.

* * *

The room was silent. C and Doc froze in place, a needle primed in Doc's hand. The man behind the counter leaned out the window. James tipped over, blood flowing from the back of his head and pooling on the ground. There was a painting of brain matter on the wall behind him. This moment, maybe four seconds, felt like an hour.

C was furious. "Everyone keep moving, we don't have time."

Doc leaned toward Michael on the table and showed him the needle. He tensed up and started squirming, tried to roll off the table, and was quickly returned to his back.

"This is only a little bit of ketamine and fentanyl like they use in the hospital, it will not kill you, it's just going to knock you out for a little. Should wear off in about an hour." Michael breathed heavily as C secured his forearm. Doc put the needle into the skin on the inside of his elbow and pulled back the plunger. A cloud of dark blood bloomed in the syringe—a beautiful sight that he never got tired of. He pushed the plunger and the mixture chased itself down through the needle. Michael tensed every muscle in his body. Hoping that he could create enough back pressure to push the drug out.

After a few moments, the effects were felt; he became drowsy. His eyes rolled around, nystagmus set in. He fought ferociously in his mind, trying to keep his subconscious above the water. But he was going to drown in it. Ketamine is a hell of a drug. The last thing he saw was the gleam of light off a silver scalpel as C placed a tourniquet around his arm. Doc made a clean, two-inch incision, lengthwise, along the man's wrist. Blood oozed out, bright and red. There, sitting on the vein, like a small pill, oblong and black with small orange light, was the PII.

Doc moved quickly. He dropped the scalpel and was handed a pair of forceps. The PII was connected to the vein. He clamped off the vessel just below the PII. Back again with the scalpel and a pair of tweezers, he cut around the implant. Dark blood started seeping out. With a final cut, he pulled out the black pill and turned to C. In C's hand was a small rectangular device, about the size of a pack of cigarettes, a little shorter and thicker. The bottom half was black and the top was a clear plastic square dome. Inside the dome was blood that C had collected with a large-bore syringe when the vein was cut. A top lid flipped open and Doc dropped the PII in the blood. Lights on the front of the device were flashing rhythmically. The number "120" was displayed on a screen in the center below a small power switch and two arrows. Doc quickly set down his instruments and picked up what almost looked like a taser with a metal rod sticking out of the end. He focused the rod at the vein where he had removed the PII and pressed a button. A blue electric arc sprung from the tip, bright and exact. It burned the vein, cauterizing it. Doc removed the forceps and C pinched the skin together. He burned the incision leaving a clean scar, a concession for the nice businessman who had done so well.

C brought the blood-filled device to the man behind the counter.

"T, are you ready? We're gettin' close." C set the device on the counter and plugged it in.

"Yeah, I'm good. Pack up. I'm sending it through now." T typed away at the keyboard. Initiating a transaction to move all funds from the businessman's bank accounts to a program on the cube—a mini bank of sorts. Doc wrapped up his blood-covered tools and threw them in his bag. He and G grabbed the ends of the metal sheets that still held Michael's limp body and pulled hard, slowly forcing them back to a straight sheet. Doc and G headed for the door grabbing the "Closed" sign on the way out. C looked at his watch and waited for T who was now staring at the computer, waiting.

"Two seconds." A ding sounded from the computer.

"There's always time to eject properly," T said like an old-school house teacher providing a sagely mantra. "Wouldn't want to lose everything with a corrupted file." He pulled all the wires, shoved them in his bag with the power cube, and threw himself over the counter. His foot caught on the glass and he tumbled over himself, landing on his back.

"Ugh. Graceful." He coughed and C pulled him to his feet. He leaned back through the window and bid adieu to the counter girl, flashing a "call me" sign. C grabbed his arm and dragged him out of the bank. Above the door, he pulled a small paddle of wood out from between the magnetic locks. His head snapped back, taking one last look at the man bleeding against the wall, who lay there, hole in face, hand on phone. At least he died a hero.

Michael's gold watch ticked, 12:06.

2 | ORGANIZING

(Four years ago)

C paced his garage, reorganizing tools and screws into crates and drawers. The center of the room was taken up by a large work table lined with etched-in rulers and protractors. He grabbed a piece of wood from the ground and tossed it on the table where the ruler lit up underneath it. A small display at one end gave an exact measurement of the span of board that covered it. Holes for clamp arms and tools dotted the surface and the slit for a table saw ran along one side. The sides were flat board with sectional creases that swung up and over to produce a table-mounted drill press, band saw, and miter saw. Just right of center, a square lifted to reveal a planer, and left of the center rose a multilevel sander. The top of the market versions had a Bot that could rise and store the different tools from an interface on the surface that would also track blade ware and could order parts from an internal store. C had invested in a few early models so he had to manually flip each tool out, but the table would change out blades and bits with the right commands.

One wall of the shop was lined with hooks that hung hand tools and baskets meticulously gridded out and taped off. On the opposite wall was a fastener dispenser. C opened the face of the dispenser and reloaded a slot of one-and-a-half-inch wood screws from a box. He closed the face and punched buttons to add the count to the inventory. It was not nearly the newest version, but it worked most of the time. In the corner, he checked the dust container on his vacuum Bot, a four-foot shop vac that tracked the air density around his hands and placed a wide mouth suction hose in the most ideal spot to catch sawdust and metal shavings. He dumped the container in the trash and replaced it. A cased wrench set sat on top of a counter, open with pieces strewn about laying on top of each other. C pressed the sockets back in their slots with a satisfying pop and locked the case closed. He opened the bottom cabinet and set the box in the middle section of a three-level shelving system and paused.

The bottom shelf was empty, though, on inspection, the back wall of that section was only half as deep. C checked his watch and stuck a hand up under the shelf where the rear wall of the bottom cubby met the top. His fingers felt for a small crease somewhere around three inches from the left side. He gave a small push and a square cube dropped into his hand. He ran the back of the cube along the right side of the back wall until a magnet caught and something deep in the construction clicked. With a press of the right edge, the wall swung out revealing a hidden compartment behind the false back.

C pulled out the contents and placed them on the table, three odd-looking metal components, two were still wrapped in plastic, and one looked more worn. It had been a while since he had last seen his old partner, Ed. These Bot parts were from their last pull. C picked up the worn one and rolled it around in his hands, inspecting the pieces. It was heavy, dense. During the automated revolution, these computers were hot commodities. The company they both worked for produced high-end Bots and parts. Replacing a personal Bot's computer—or heart—with one of these was like throwing a Hellcat Hemi in a Camry.

C worked on the operations side, scheduling and organizing calls and employees. When their head mechanic left he made a phone call and brought in Ed.

Six months ago, Ed had dropped by with these parts. "This one was only used in a prototype Bot that was testing a new knee joint. They were scrapping the body and I snagged the Heart from the workbench. The other two I got from the delivery room. My guy down there hooked it up."

Every few weeks Ed would show up with parts or tools from the shop that he lifted from the job or his friend in the package center and they would sit in C's garage for a few months until the company had filed the insurance for losses and the pieces were long forgotten. Then the two of them would drive out of town to the next state over and sell them off to one of Ed's old buddies that dealt in backroom Bots—smart weapons systems, personal bodyguards, things the mainstream robotics companies were legally barred from. It was an easy operation that was started to keep up with the new onslaught of hospital bills that had been stacking up in C's inbox. He stared at the pieces on the table, not knowing what to do with them now that Ed was MIA again. The sound of a car rolling up the driveway broke his trance. He checked his watch, "shit."

The garage door was half-closed, but he could see the front bumper creep up to the top of the asphalt. He grabbed the three Bot hearts and threw them back into the hidden compartment, shutting the door and replacing the magnet. The car door slammed. Low-heeled shoes clacked up to the door and four fingers wrapped under the rubber seal. The garage door floated up silently, revealing a woman, tall, blonde, with sharp features and a loose blouse.

"I thought I saw a shadow in here." She spoke with a dark voice. Someone who was good at commanding a room, or whispering in ears.

"Hey." C covered his brow to narrow the light from the setting sun through the open garage door. He looked past her to the car. "Where's Charlie?"

"The lab was taking a while to get results back and the doctor wanted to keep him one more night for observation."

C let out a deep breath and rolled his head back. "El, I don't know if we can afford another night."

"I know, I know. He had another coughing fit this morning so they wanted to continue the breathing treatment for just a little longer."

C rubbed at his forehead. "Alright. Are you going back tonight?"

"No, they told me I should head home and come by in the morning."

"I can go over tomorrow morning and get him. You take the day."

"Are you sure? You were there for the last three days."

"Yeah, I want to talk to the doctor about his prognosis and see if we can get these breathing treatments at home."

El nodded. They hung in silence. She ran her eyes around the shop and twisted a thin smile. "It looks good in here." C returned a light tip of the head. "Did you have dinner?"

"No, I'm not hungry."

"Okay, well I'm going to make something if you change your mind." El turned on her heel and walked through the door into the house. C sat and stared at the cabinet with the Hearts. She found out about their operation towards the end when her curiosity about the influx of money was answered by a series of late-night phone calls and rumored stories of theft at the company picnic. Safe to say she was not excited about the whole situation but now, with Ed gone, she relaxed more. The two of them were as amicable as lions and hyenas in adjacent cages at the zoo. If she saw the Hearts in the shop, there would be a conversation he wasn't ready to have. He dusted off his hands and did a final check around the shop before following behind.

3 | Out

C and T ran down the steps of the bank and got into a clean white van that was sitting on the street. The other two had already made themselves comfortable, strapped in, ready to go. There were two benches on either side and an array of toolboxes in the middle. A nice setup for a team of handymen, in case anyone asked. Doc was sitting on the far side bench and G in the driver's seat. T pulled himself through the side door and C jumped into the passenger seat. They pulled off their headlamps. Sirens could be heard in the distance. The second the door hit the latch, they were off. It was a mild getaway, five mph over the speed limit. Far too many movies made that mistake and C was smarter than that; they eased down the road. The stolen plates were more than enough to get pulled over, but it wouldn't be long before they were undercover.

"What the fuck was that!?" C was on a full rampage. He ripped his mask off and threw it at the dash. "Did he have a gun?"

"He was calling the cops!" G tried to defend himself, knowing full well he fucked up.

"What!? Did he have a gun!?"

"I didn't see one, but he was literally on the phone with the police."

"We can deal with the police! That's why we cut the

power supply and do this thing in four goddamn minutes!" C looked like he was about to start throwing punches. T put a hand on his seat belt buckle, ready to intervene if things went south. "We do not shoot innocent people! We don't shoot anyone unless they have a gun and are PHYSICALLY POINTING IT at one of us! So why? Please explain to me, why the fuck that guy has a bullet in his head." Spit flew out of his mouth as he spoke.

"I was aiming for the phone." G pouted and glanced out the window at the mirror.

"You were aiming for the phone that he was holding in front of his face? Does that make any sense to you? And what was the deal with the security guard?"

"I was just trying to intimidate."

"Intimidate!? YOU HAVE A GUN! That's it! Yell and scream all you want, wave that big black pea shooter around, and call it a fucking day. We're not here to beat up fat security guards, and we are sure as fuck not here to kill anyone."

G was silent. He pressed on the gas as a light turned green.

They had driven about a mile when they pulled into a parking lot under a bridge. A large box truck sat in a parking spot in the middle of the lot. It was wheelless, sitting on four jack stands. G hit a button on the visor above him. The back door of the box truck lifted like a garage door, pulling up a section of the rear bumper with it. Inside, there was nothing, no axles, no cab, no engine. It was hollow all the way to the grill where light shined through. G reached out his window and grabbed his side-view mirror, which popped off easily, and tossed it in the back of the van. C did the same on his side. The van drove into the back of the truck, slowly; it was a tight fit. Metal banged and clicked, there was a mechanical whir, and all of a sudden the truck frame lifted. It clamped down, resting on the roof rack, and in passing looked more or less like a normal box truck, or at least, not like a white van. The whole process only took about ten seconds and once the frame lifted off the stands, they could start moving. The back door closed as they drove off, revealing license plates properly registered and up to date.

* * *

They pulled up to a warehouse in the middle of an industrial yard. Other box trucks, bigger and smaller, sat around the lot. "Collis Logistics" and "Modern Moving" took up the units to the left and right. They were large companies with buildings that stretched far to either side. Companies that the dead man at True North might have a hand in. Well, had. The faces of the units were drab. Brown and red with limited windows, as if the architect sketched the building on a napkin from a fast food restaurant and the contractor took the color of the napkin to heart. Still, the sign for "Modern Moving" lit up at night and that's about as much as one could ask from a trucking company in a napkin-colored building.

The unit in the middle was small, very small. It was most likely supposed to be a storefront or customer service for the neighboring units but the building's owner decided to spin a quick buck and lease it out to a guy who kept to himself and seemed to do mechanical work on small box trucks. It did come with a nice-sized bay, so that was convenient.

The crew pulled into the garage next to the front door, maybe meant to be a showroom for cars or machines; it was deeper than it looked on the outside. The van-in-the-truck parked to the right in the far corner and the back door of the truck rose. The van's rear door swung open and the crew hopped out one by one, bringing the equipment, bags, and boxes, through a door to the right, into what looked like a back alley lounge. A dirty orange couch sat along the left wall facing a round wooden table and chairs that took up the majority of the center of the room. On the wall opposite the door from the garage stood a large gun safe, dark mottled gray with an electric keypad and a backup hard key lock. In the right corner sat a high bar and shelves with miscellaneous gear. C placed a toolbox from the van on the ground and unloaded a collection of scuba gear, masks and oxygen tanks onto the counter. The rest of the crew dumped their gear on the center table and started opening bags. C punched in a code on the safe and swung open the quarter-ton door as the crew cleaned and returned the equipment to its place. T walked in, laptop in hand, and sat down on the couch to continue his work.

"G, can I talk to you outside?" C stood near the front door that led to the parking lot. G put down the metal sheet he was cleaning and trudged out.

It had started drizzling and dark clouds were rolling in. G looked dismissive, his arms folded, looking nowhere in particular. C was more decisive. He moved with a purpose, setting himself between G and the building.

"What?" G spat. It wasn't much of a question.

"What do you mean, 'what?'" C looked him in the eye. "What are you trying to do here?" G didn't answer. "This is supposed to be easy. It's been rehearsed. The lines are

31

written, the movement is blocked. We have a very small window of time and every time you do something fucking stupid, it gets smaller. This is the second time you've shot someone unnecessarily and the fourth time we've had this talk."

"I thought the first guy had a gun!" G tried to justify his past actions again as if the case hadn't already been deliberated and picked apart.

"He was sixteen and he was there with his mother!"

"I only hit his arm." G rubbed his forehead with his palm, defending himself for the hundredth time.

"That's not the point. You've been a bull in a china shop on almost every mission. We kept you 'cause…" C squinted, looking into G's eyes. They were bloodshot around the edges and had a light glaze over the top. "Are you doped up right now?"

"No."

"Are you fuckin' kidding me? Did you go in like that?"

"I'm fine."

"You're fine? Your pupils are like dinner plates." C leaned in closer to inspect his face. "You got fuckin' shit in your nostril."

G threw both of his hands out at C's chest and gave a hard shove. "Fuck off, man."

C stumbled backward. He thought about returning the gesture but shook it off instead. "You're out." He turned around and started to walk away.

"What do you mean, I'm out? You can't kick me out! You can't do this operation without me!"

"We'll figure it out," C called over his shoulder. G ran at him, chest to back, bear-hugging him on the way down. The rain picked up.

"What the fuck are you doing!?" C rolled over. G got a hold of the front of his shirt and swung a punch, catching a good piece of jaw. It was a solid strike, and it hurt. C scrambled to stand up as G pulled at his shirt. C grabbed his arm and twisted it outward, sliding a foot behind G's. With a hard punch to the chest, G lost his balance and went down. C was stronger and bigger, but G was wild, his eyes reeling. He hit the ground hard and tried to roll out left but C was on him. G kicked and twisted. Landing a foot in C's side and a fist upper cutting into his nose. C backed off for a second to recuperate, feeling the pain and pushing it down. G tried to stand, feeling good about himself, ready to keep going, but C was done playing. He grabbed G by the chest and pushed him back down before he could get on two feet. He held him there, knees on arms, feet on pelvis. Three good strikes to the face and two to the ribs. C stumbled as he stood. G rolled on the ground in pain. The final kick to the ribs might have been too much, but there was a point to make. G pulled himself to his feet. The rain was coming down hard. Blood mixed with the water and oil, iridescent in the crevices of the asphalt.

"Fine, fuck you and fuck this. You'll fuckin' pay. Don't worry, you'll fuckin' pay." He limped off holding his side.

C hobbled to the door, arm covering his side, bleeding from the nose. His head spun. A clock started, cosmic and foreboding. "We'll figure it out." "You'll fuckin' pay." The altercation bounced around in space. *Was this the end of the game? Can we pull this off without a fourth guy? Without security? A driver? A lookout?*

The operation was so perfect. Every second accounted for. They had rehearsed it over and over. The best they ever did was three and a half minutes; the police response time was usually five to six depending on who on the street noticed a group of four masked men run into the bank, but they could get unlucky. It didn't make him comfortable. It was one less person to split the money with, but if they were too slow, if the hero had a gun… He pushed open the door which took more energy than he wanted it to.

"Holy shit, dude!" Doc dropped the scalpel. He jogged over to C who shooed him off. "What do you need? I have a med kit in the truck." He sprinted towards the garage.

"I'm alright, just a bloody nose. I'll be fine." Doc had left the room in search of supplies.

"Damn, man. We could barely hear you guys over the rain. We would have come out. What happened?" T had gotten up and was standing at the table.

"G is out." C sat down. He let out a long breath, not realizing that he had been holding it.

"Probably for the best." T grabbed a beer from the mini-fridge next to the couch and set it down on the table.

"Thanks." C opened the can and took a swig.

"What are we going to do? Is he going to turn us in?"

"He doesn't know our names. He's just a riled up dope-head. He'll go stomping around for a while, get high, and forget about it." Doc returned with the first aid kit and took a knee next to the chair. C shoved a ball of cotton up his nose and Doc put a Steri-Strip on his split lip. He lifted his shirt and Doc did a quick evaluation to make sure there wasn't anything internal.

"It looks alright. Might have broken a rib at the bottom there. We'll keep an eye on it. Do you want a half dose of fentanyl?"

"No, I'll be alright."

"Are you sure? I can put it in the saline lock." He

gestured to the bump on C's arm under his sleeve.

"Really, I'm good." He gave an appreciative smile and dropped a hand on Doc's shoulder. C's phone vibrated. His hand snapped to his pocket as though he'd been shot. He pulled out the phone and looked at it, half-knowing who it was going to be and what she wanted.

"I'll be back in a second." C stood up. It was a slow motion with a few grunts and a lot of grimacing. Doc put a hand on his back. It was really there more for motivation than anything. C pulled his head up and straightened his back. He was still the leader of this group and sure as hell was going to look like it. He walked to the door, taking each step like nothing had ever been wrong. He was strong like that, able to push aside all his pain to carry on; it would probably kill him one day.

The rain had broken up. There was a mist in the air, the kind after a heavy summer monsoon when the smell of oil lifts from the asphalt. There was a heat, like something in the core of the earth went into overdrive for a brief moment, and you were catching the end of it. It radiated from the ground and stuck to the skin. C's phone was vibrating in his hand, though it seemed like it was coming from everywhere at once, shaking his body, his mind. He stiffened up and took a breath. His side hurt as he inhaled, the accessory muscles pulling on a most likely fractured tenth rib.

"Hello?," he answered. It's a strange thing, the way we say hello sometimes, knowing full well who is on the other end of the line, but pretending like we don't. Like trying to hold on to the mystery of telephonic communication before caller ID. Maybe we just want people to think we are important enough to forget them.

"Are you coming tomorrow?" The voice was from a woman, dark and determined, sure of the answer but needing to ask the question anyway—the desire to maintain some semblance of control.

"Yes." C tried to hold his breath when he spoke so as not to sound like the wounded animal he was. He didn't do a very good job at it. The phone echoed every time he spoke into it. It only happened when he stood near the building. He assumed there was some interference with all the radio equipment in the surrounding industrial park.

"Okay, I'll see you at eight." She hung up. He stood there with his phone against his head for far longer than it needed to be. A light breeze came through and immediately cured him of all his pain, lifting him off the ground a little, channeling the heat of the earth into his chest, and cooling his skin. Then again, maybe it was just her voice. He put his phone in his pocket and limped back to the door. C straightened his back, pursed his broken lip, and pushed on through.

4 | PETITIONS

The office was furnished by someone who was hired to decorate offices and was on their first job. IKEA and knock-off Restoration Hardware sponsored the room, vomiting both sleek and rustic accents sporadically around the space. It looked ambiguously nice. The furniture was an array of either dark-stained wood or shiny white laminate which was an interesting choice considering the ocean blue carpet. Blue is a calming color. "It keeps a peace with the greater world around us, a divine hug from both the sky and sea right in the presence of your home or office," or something along those lines hung on the tag when the carpet was purchased. The decorator was going for a look, perhaps a series of mood boards, one explaining the serenity of blue planes, one describing the warmth of stained wood furniture, and a third claiming that shiny white accents bring a reviving freshness to the workspace. These pieces were not intended to be used together, but dammit if she didn't give it her all.

A large wooden desk sat in the center, closer to the back wall. On it sat a collection of desk toys that somebody saw in a movie once. In the two back corners of the room stood large wooden stands that held glistening white pots filled with spilling ivy. Plastic ivy. The staff had tried planting real ivy but it quickly died because no one in the office was going to allow "plant waterer" to become part of their job description—the women feared the inevitable death, the men could not bring themselves to that level of commitment, and the cleaning crew charged extra for it. Along the walls hung pictures of nothing in particular—abstract blue lines on white canvases. Remarkably, the decorator had matched the blue in the paintings to the blue of the carpet which was, by far, the most impressive thing that they had ever accomplished. In front of the desk sat two wooden chairs with white knit cushions that were much too overstuffed. The chairs were canted towards each other at an angle that a focus group somewhere had come up with to maximize the amount of emotional connection between the chair sitters while still providing a safe area for a third party to jump in, should the choking start.

Behind the desk was a man in his late forties, balding to the point that he might as well shave it off and at least look like a dignified chairman of a country club. But he was committed to the fringe of brown and gray fuzz that nuzzled up against the sides of his head, like bumpers on a bowling lane. We all have to hold on to something. He wore a black suit that was habitually too fancy for the occasion; his light pink shirt and bright red tie comically toppled the already-tipping scale of color balance that the room was trying to hold on to. He was a nice man, doing his best at a job that took an interesting mix of psychology, law, and math. At the front edge of his desk, in front of the toy collection, there was a wooden plaque with his name engraved above the words Carlo Law, Divorce Attorneys.

C knocked on the door and entered at the same time. His face was still badly beaten from the day before but the swelling had mostly gone down. An impressive bruise ran along the left side of his face and his nose was almost crooked. He was slightly hunched as he came in, trying to stand straight; he had lost any adrenaline that was keeping the rib injury mild and was now sore when he stretched it. The lawyer gasped as he came in. The sight was something he had not seen in person since a rough night in college many years ago, as there was not much hand-to-hand combat in the world of modern law. Maybe a few hundred years ago things in the judicial world were more interesting. He pondered this for a minute as C took a seat, delicately.

El was sitting in the seat next to him, straight-backed with her legs crossed at the knee. Her hair was blonde and long. It hung straight and curled toward the bottom as if it had grown in a slow-motion bounce off her shoulders and then tumbled off. She was wearing a white blouse, floral and lace, with short sleeves and a high mock-neck collar. Her legs were wrapped in straight black pants that billowed when the wind blew and she flexed her toes in flat shoes; her 5'11" frame forbade her from wearing heels. Her arms were bare, pale, deliberate in their placement. A wedding ring sat around her finger though she twisted it a lot, sliding it on and off with her pinky and thumb.

"What the hell happened to you?" Her dark voice muted and pressed. It spat mostly anger but somewhere, in the back of the throat, there was a slight inflection of concern.

"Nothing, I'm alright." He gestured an invitation to start the meeting and forget the view.

"You are not alright. Your face is a mess. Did you get in a fight?"

"Car ran a stop sign and hit me on the crosswalk. Just

a little banged up. The driver took off. New car, no plates." He was reading lines off the back wall of the office.

She looked at him suspiciously, but there was hesitation in her attack. She closed her eyes and took a deep breath, focusing her attention now on the lawyer, periodically checking in on C.

"Thank you both for coming in today. Would you like something to drink, sir?"

It took a second for C to realize he was talking to him. "Oh, uh, sure. Water would be good." His healing had left his body persistently dehydrated.

The lawyer pressed a button on his desk and a few seconds later a Bot rolled into the room. It had a cylindrical base and a single robotic arm with a four-fingered hand at the end.

"Water, for our guest, please," the lawyer called. With a muted whirring, the Bot opened a hatch on the front of its base and pulled out a metal pitcher of water. Simultaneously a cup rose from the top. The arm poured a precise glass, replacing the pitcher and moving the cup to the desk in front of C.

"There are some things that need to be discussed and some papers signed." The lawyer flipped through the stack on his desk, then opened a drawer, rummaging but not finding them quickly. C sat motionless, blinking slowly, breathing slower.

"Elizabeth, you are petitioning, correct?" Finally, he pulled out a piece of paper from under a stack that he had checked before and gave a confirming smile.

"Yes, that's correct." She snapped into business mode.

"And you are signing a No-Fault under…" He read the document that he had partially prepared. "Irreconcilable differences?" Elizabeth nodded.

"And are you signing for Voluntary Appearance, or did you want to deliberate?" He stared at C with a look of servitude. They could have done this online but Elizabeth wanted to make a point out of it.

"Voluntary." C did not make eye contact. If he did then he would exist. He was trapped in a Samuel Beckett film. The lawyer placed the papers on the table.

"Okay, I'm going to need you to both read and sign these. This is just the preliminary petition." He sat back in his chair, removing himself from their world, allowing the process to take place.

Elizabeth reached forward and picked up the paperwork. She skimmed through, trying to remain emotionless and took the expensive fountain pen from the holder on the edge of the desk—a writing instrument that the lawyer seemed to be proud of. She signed her name and handed the pen to C. With a calculated shift in weight, he scribbled his name on the paper and dropped the pen on the desk where it made a resonant thud. The lawyer shuttered and grabbed it quickly, like a phone dropped in a puddle, praying that it was not scratched. He tried to not make a big deal of it but his eyes betrayed him.

The meeting carried on. C sat, mostly in silence, nodding occasionally or answering in limited words. He would rather have been arrested yesterday than come to this. He watched the papers turn and the pens dance. It was a bad dream that he couldn't shake. More than once he poked his bruised cheek, trying to elicit enough pain to wake himself up but it only hurt more. He wanted to fight it, to walk out of the room and drag her with him. Give her a kiss and walk home hand-in-hand, forgetting all the trouble he'd been in. That wasn't going to happen. He was too far in with his crew and he couldn't return to normal life. It was too painful and memories haunted him like figures in a dark room. He still couldn't gauge how serious she was, after all of the threats; he was already living in a separate apartment, but now, paying for a lawyer seemed to be a new turn.

They left the office, each with a folder of papers. Elizabeth walked with a power to her, almost a strut, not that this was an easy call, but, like everything else in her life, she was good at persevering without reflection. An instinct meant for wounded animals to maintain strength in the face of a predator, regardless of condition. Once in the hallway, they stopped. Her glow had diminished after the door was closed. She looked at C like a stray dog who bit a hornet's nest. There was disappointment and fear, anger and uneasiness, sympathy and resoluteness. She was always so good at confusing him. He hung his head, scratched his ear, waiting for the okay. Waiting for her to put a hand on his back, run her fingers through his hair, kiss him on the forehead. But it wouldn't happen.

"I'll see you next week?" She was cold. It had to be a defense mechanism.

"El, can we stop and talk for a minute?" He was having a hard time standing, his head was a pressure cooker.

"Talk about what? Why you showed up twenty minutes late looking like you fell in a trash compactor? Sure, let's talk." She had no idea about the bank operations, but she knew there was something.

"I told you, I had a hit and run." He said it dryly, knowing it was a lie but sticking to it like a fly in a trap. She looked him in the eyes, something she hadn't done in a long time. This was going to be the closest he was going to get. Two universes waving in parallel, marginally bumping every hundred million years or so. This was one of them.

"Why? Why won't you help me?" She held her face firm, her eyes asking more than her mouth.

"I," he hesitated. "I'm trying. I don't…"

"You're trying? You haven't said more than a few words in months." She hit hard. "You're late to meetings, you've made no attempt to come back and work things out, every counseling session we had you stared at the wall and then complained about how much it was costing. For a year and a half you've been absent."

The hallway hung in the echo of her battering. C hung his head and rubbed his face lightly avoiding the bruising.

She looked at him pathetically, but her eyes shifted to pity.

"What do you want?" She softened.

"What?"

"Do you want to go back or do you want this?" She held up the papers.

"Of course, I want to go back. I just…" He grasped for the words to use. He wanted more than anything for everything to go back to normal but he couldn't bring himself to it mentally. When he tried, his mind would spiral down to darkness and fear, like he was drowning. The profits from the robberies were the only thing keeping him afloat mentally.

"Figure it out."

C looked at her and furrowed his eyes.

"Go to therapy or get some medication, for god's sake, go see a doctor about your face." She waved the paperwork

in the air. "I'm not fucking around anymore, you understand?" There was a brief step into her anger before she
pulled back. "You get one more." She pointed with the
corner of the rolled paper. "One more chance to bring
this around. Go do whatever you have to do, see whom-
ever you have to see, and if you can show me legitimate
improvement then we will start moving backward from
this." She gestured lazily to the lawyer's door. "If not…"
She shrugged, offering up whatever he could imagine.

With a spin of the heel, she was off. He tried to call
after her, but he choked on it. Besides, he didn't have anything to say. He just wanted her to look in his eyes again.

5 | ODE TO SLEEP

C returned home. He turned right off the sidewalk and up the front stairs of his apartment building. Further up the sidewalk, a Bot swept trash out to the street while an automated truck drove along the curb and scooped up the bags and other debris. C bought the loft apartment about a year ago when he needed to put his share of the Crew's money somewhere—and his wife had made it clear that he should stay somewhere else for a while. It was near the city center, a little off the beaten path, and not in the wholly nice part of town. Reminiscent of the brownstones of New York, the building was crammed between two other buildings, owned by other people with other ghosts. He walked up the four flights to the loft entrance. There was an elevator, but he decided at some point that the extra cardio would make up for the gym that he didn't go to. He was rather fit, so he supposed it was working.

The main staircase ended on the third floor and a gate guarded the remaining steps to the fourth. He paused at the top to take a breath. His ribs ached and his heart beat harder than it should have. In retrospect, the elevator would have been welcomed, but he persevered, refusing to let a fight with some punk kid dictate his life. He placed his wrist against the scanner and the gate let out a clang of the bolt flipping over. He slid the gate to the right and let the spring bring it back where it locked itself. At the top of the stairs was a short hallway leading to his door. He had put a small table and plant there one day when he was feeling domestic. He unlocked the knob and the deadbolt with an old-fashioned key and walked in. If there was one thing he knew about electric locks and safeguards, they could all be hacked.

It was not the most beautiful apartment in the city, but there were a lot of nice things in it—things that could be bought for cash without raising suspicion. Paper cash, for all intents and purposes, had become mostly unused. It existed, and if someone went to a bank they could pull some out. A few very remote towns and businesses still circulated it, and it remained the government's only federally-recognized currency. But after the PII gained popularity, there was an underground movement that very quickly became not so underground: Angiocoin. Cryptocurrencies had been around for a long time but Angiocoin was the wave that took it to the general public. At a time when everything was becoming more and more carefully tracked by both large corporations and governments, the populace wanted a digital cash that could be used virtually anywhere and be unmonitored. The difference between Angiocoin and the other cryptos was that it was not backed by some obscure code mining. It was backed with real U.S. dollars. The units shifted with the economy and each Angiocoin was exactly one to one with a dollar which made it feel very stable—that was, of course, still a point of contention amongst the talking heads and economists. When Angiocoin announced that it would be integrating with the PII, the country flocked. Most people already had the tiny device implanted in their wrist. It was used for personal records, identity information, and transactions with traditional money. But now that it could transfer money as quietly as cash and as efficiently as a debit card, it became the gold standard overnight.

The company behind Angiocoin ran an enormous bank on a massive server that held dozens of trillions of dollars in real digital money in a few billion accounts, both personal and commercial. It was the largest bank in the world, full of electrified cash. It had developed its own loan and credit system, its own ledger and reporting, and it was growing bigger every day, expanding to other countries.

Money is just a concept whether physical or digital. If the Federal Reserve printed a billion unbacked dollars and put them in circulation, the local pizza joint would accept them just the same. But in this new world, dominated by Angiocoin, once a dollar was deposited it immediately disappeared from federal circulation and resurfaced as Angiocoin in an encrypted account ready for encrypted transactions. It could pay the energy bill online, purchase a house, or buy cocaine in the alley. Privately owned and hidden, and the best part for the general public was that the government had no authority over it. Tax season was a nightmare.

But no taxes meant no tax revenue for Uncle Sam. The rise of untracked digital transactions meant the Feds were missing out on trillions of tax dollars and they started facing a real financial crisis. So, they stepped in to do what they do best: bureaucracy. The government integrated itself into every bank chain and all traditional monetary transactions over a minimum amount had to be reported so they could be heavily taxed in a last ditch effort to stop its revenue stream from bleeding out. For the time being, that minimum was fairly high, and most of the lower class didn't mind. But, little by little, the taxable threshold minimum was dropping and people were getting uneasy. The popular "tax the rich" movement was becoming "tax only the rich."

The new laws meant that all stock, bond, and equity market transactions had to be signed for in person, exclusively by the person performing it, and the transaction could only take place at a government-authorized bank. All major corporations valued over another minimum threshold were required to report regular financial records to the government to prove they weren't hiding copious amounts of money in crypto. A whole industry of compliance officers, lawyers, and bureaucrats grew like weeds. With the federal bank in a tailspin, class warfare escalated. The lower class continued to dump all their money into Angiocoin to avoid taxes and fees. They believed in it wholeheartedly as the future of money and were sure that it had become too big to fail. The rich, on the other hand, clung to their traditional dollars, scared that one of two things would happen. Either Angiocoin would be a passing fad and in ten years everyone who invested money in it would have nothing of value, or it would continue to rise until the government got fed up and started imposing legal regulations on it, devaluing it drastically. So, the rich hoarded their American dollars. Besides, basically all market transactions still happened in real money and most of the upper class's wealth was tied up in bonds and stock options anyway.

* * *

The door of C's bachelor apartment opened into the

living room. A large beige sectional took up the middle of the room—an island that everything else orbited around. Across from it sat a small wooden credenza with glass doors, modern and specific. It was dwarfed by the absolutely monumental television mounted on the wall above it. Eighty inches in diagonal—a feat of mankind that seemed, impossibly, to float on the wall with such magnitude and excellence. On the credenza sat a long soundbar, black and silver, casting signals to both the subwoofer under the couch and the satellite speakers that stood on stands at either side. A movie theater would blush. Everything else in the room seemed secondary to the setup. Behind the couch, along the wall, was a desk that pressed up against the corner between the living room and the archway that led to the kitchen. It may as well have been one room, but the fifteen-foot-wide arch between the two sections gave it a nice frame.

C sat down at the desk and tapped his fingers on an empty section of wood to the left of the keyboard. A six-by-six-inch square of light flashed to life under his hand. A desktop computer, as impressive as the TV, woke up showing a login window with a blinking cursor which moved as he dragged his finger over the light square. He wrapped his hand around the right side of the screen, stretching his fingers along the back. They fell into place, four fingerprint scanners, grooved out and smooth, lifting his identity from his skin and offering it to the system as collateral. The login window disappeared. Behind it stood the website of True North National Bank and a collection of pictures of the lobby that he found from some internet review. He could see the spot where the man who was shot had tried to be a hero. No blood splatter, just cement and tile. Another man's feet stood in the same spot. The wrong place at the wrong time.

C quit out of all the open pages and sat back. He stared ahead, unmoving, unconsciously holding his breath. On the screen sat a picture, made more dramatic by the sheer size of the monitor. It was a picture of him and his wife on a boardwalk from their vacation to Los Angeles. He was wearing a goofy-looking hat. At the time, he thought it looked pretty hip, despite the passing criticism from Elizabeth. He was in a white collared button-up shirt with tiny palm trees and beige shorts. El was glowing; she wore the same white lace top that he had just seen her in at the lawyer's office, her hair curled and blonde. They were smiling, happy, so unaware of what would become of them. C closed his eyes and remembered. When he looked back up he focused on the center of the picture. Standing between him and his wife was a boy—head tilted up and missing a couple of teeth; his smile radiated. His eyes were nearly closed, trying to block out the bright sun. He wore a bright red shirt with a silhouetted broken print of a palm tree on it. "Look, Dad, we're matching!" C dug as far as he could into his brain, desperately trying to remember every second of that day.

His meditation was disturbed by movement coming from the kitchen floor. He turned his head cautiously, mindful of his pain. Around the corner, a bright orange furry head popped out to survey the room and investigate who had walked in. "Hey, girl." He stood up and walked toward her. The cat stepped out further, decidedly comfortable with the situation, rubbing her side on the corner of the wall. He bent over and grabbed her by the belly, lifting her up and holding her like a baby, cradled. She looked around from the new vantage point, then sniffed his face and rubbed her cheek on his nose. A car without a muffler drove past outside, the driver inserting his gargantuan penis into the lives of the people around him. C scratched at his kitten's belly, her fur warm and wispy. She looked down, calculating the distance, timing her rollout. He flipped her over and set her down, legs and toes extended ready for impact.

Through the archway, C moved to the stove to heat a shiny silver tea kettle and walked into the bathroom to rummage around under the sink. He pulled out an ACE wrap and a hot water bottle and returned to the kitchen, leaving both things on the granite-covered island that took up the center of the room. He swung open the fridge, also massive and impressive with its shimmering glass and brushed stainless steel. It was full of wrapped meats and beer—well-stocked for the cliché man living alone. The bottom drawers held bags of vegetables. A red bell pepper stood out among the green. C grabbed a loaf of bread, a package of sliced turkey and cheese, and a bottle of mustard and walked to the couch. Setting the food on the black wooden coffee table, he hit a button on a touch screen built into the arm of the couch. The TV turned on with a surrounding and satisfying hum.

"… again, this time taking a life." A news reporter was covering the story from yesterday's operation. "Signature in the team's robberies, all power and backup power was compromised prior to the event. The four men can be seen here from security footage on an adjacent building." Four squares came on the screen, each with a zoomed-in blurry picture of the heads of him, G, T, and Doc, obscured by the bright glare of their headlamps. C examined what he could see of four faces. He could tell which one was Doc with the dark skin and G had a scar above his left eye that removed most of his brow and left him looking pretty beat, especially when the rest of his face was covered. T had been looking in the direction of the camera and the light from the headlamp glared over his face. In the bottom right corner was C. The grainy picture didn't do him justice.

"The murdered victim, James Billmen, a local executive for the national transport company Modern Moving, the reporter went on.

C felt horrible about it, but couldn't help chuckling at the irony. He didn't mind being on the news. The Crew had taken on quite a following and even inspired a couple of attempted copycat robberies though no one else had figured out how to bypass the PII security like they had. In the growing divide between the lower middle class and the elite upper class, most of the country cheered them on as they took down one hedge fund manager after the next. If they were ever really caught and prosecuted, there would be outrage and maybe even rioting. C was sure the cops probably had a binder for each of them, a wall with strings between heads and question marks and pictures of bank fronts and wrist scars, but there was a good chance the investigations were for show.

Of course, the Feds had a pressing interest, but the local police were more concerned about the aftermath of what would happen if the famous gang of "billionaire-busters" actually went behind bars. It had been over a year since they started, and they had run a good many operations. He was surprised at his luck, but the work he put into it, the discipline he expected, carried them through. "It's smarter to be lucky than it's lucky to be smart."

Other bank robbers struggled, trying to squeeze in through the nonexistent cracks left behind by decades of evolving security systems. Once the PII came out, there was attempt after attempt to crack it. Every angle had been analyzed and picked at. Hackers tried to send signals to the device to pull information to no avail. The scanners at convenience stores and banks and airports were coded to only pull the specific information that the company requested and even that took a long process of checks and securities. People tried to modify those and still, the encryption was unbreakable. There was even a foreign threat to break into the database at the implant and information upload facilities, but that failed brilliantly when the security system sent a bug back through the VPN to the hacker and put his physical location and a picture of him from his computer camera on the FBI's map. He was caught within an hour.

For all the other thieves, the focus to break a digital device was on the digital system. A mechanical crack was something new. There were of course those who even tried what C had, stealing it out of someone's wrist and keeping it alive long enough to pull the information from it. But it always shut down or they weren't able to get the PIN transfer right, or whatever. A lot of people died. C and T had figured out the recipe, invented the technology and the system. Doing it at a bank terminal with no holds, no withdrawal limits, the speed and precision—this was unparalleled.

C tapped at the touchscreen in the couch arm. The movie *The Town* picked up where he had left off. A few minutes in, the kettle went off. C walked to the kitchen and turned the knob on the stove. He filled the hot water bottle and brought it into the living room with the wrap.

Taking his shirt off was a process. He couldn't lift his left arm well so he had to wiggle his right arm out and pull the shirt around his body, leaving everything else in place. The bruise on his left side was large — black and blue with a yellow border. His lower rib was definitely fractured, at least a little. "You'll fuckin' pay" looped in his head. He held the water bottle in between his side and his bicep, wrapping the ACE bandage around his torso. The pressure on the injury was painful but the heat was a welcome feeling. It radiated past his side, up the back of his neck, and down his legs. He laid back, attempting to watch Affleck and Renner go at it, but sleep sounded better. His eyes drifted off, the score of the movie, twisting and distorting around him. Gunshots rang out, making him tense.

All of a sudden he was on a beach, his wife laughing next to him. Her smile took up her whole face and her teeth were blinding. She could outshine the stars. A jungle of flowers could not come close. A warm summer evening by a mountain lake was not as perfect. To his right, his son was digging in the sand, convinced China was only a couple of shovelfuls away. He laughed and screamed, his white-blonde hair covered in dirty sand, the way it was supposed to be. The dream went on.

6 | ALL PERFECTION IS DIRTIED

(Three Years Ago)

It's interesting that we've decided that white would be the universal color of cleanliness, a white house, white bathroom. Something that so easily shows the darkness of dirt in contrast, when maintained, can demonstrate perfection and pristineness. A paradox. The cleaner something is, the easier it is to be dirtied on an exponential scale. The floor of a restaurant is considered clean after the night crew does a quick mop job, but no one bats an eye as the cleaning team walks over the boards with their grease-covered shoes on the way out. A germaphobe might wipe down their house with disinfectant a few times a day, not thinking about the few dozen times they pick at their nose or scratch dead skin off their arm, sprinkling bacteria in tiny dust storms across their couch. Surgeons don sterile gloves in a calculated and practiced procedure, knowing that if they even remotely graze the outside, the gloves will be discarded and they must try again. This happens, of course, in the open air, where dust and fecal matter swim freely and lay in invisible blankets over our skin. Nothing is ever clean. All perfection is dirtied.

* * *

C stirred in his chair, tracing the grooves in the wood armrest with his finger, imagining the last time it was cleaned. He looked across the room, the door was open, nurses and techs hurried by, important things to do, blood sugars to take, catheters to replace. He looked up at the white speckled tile of the drop ceiling, a grid with alternating fluorescent lights. Funny enough, they made people look slightly green. *I wonder how many files said that people looked sickly when they came in.* A whiteboard was mounted next to the door, filled with patient information and daily reports. "Charlie" was written in big letters across the top, rather badly. Earlier in the stay, a nurse put him up on a chair and let him erase her handwriting and put his own. Below the name had some medical constants, O2 LPM: 2 Via NC, IV: 22g SL R (circled) AC, Fall risk: None. In the center of the ceiling was a machine connected to a track, an x- and y-axis, designed to lift the morbidly obese to their chair for feeding and back again. The strap that connected the machine to the track seemed woefully unprepared for its job. The bed took up the majority of the room; at its end was a small passageway between the footboard and a rail of cabinets for personal belongings, above which hung a TV that had a large array of movies and shows, ready for the world's damaged goods to waste away with. *Damaged goods, was that what he was?*

"Dad?," a tiny voice called out from the bed. It was crackling and tired, having just re-entered the world from some distant dream where none of this was happening.

"Hey, buddy." C moved closer to the bed and offered

up his hand. Charlie shuffled his arm out from under the blankets and placed his fingers onto his father's. C inspected his son's hand. The creases matched his. Charlie stretched his back out, letting out a small cough that grew for a split second and then settled.

"Can we have waffles for breakfast? I haven't had waffles in, like, a million weeks." The boy's eyes were not all the way open, but the bright blue of the iris was glistening through the crack in his eyelids. He looked out the door as an alarm went off somewhere. "Old man on the move." He quoted his father's default line and laughed carefully, being sure not to start up coughing again. C laughed too.

"Of course we can have waffles. How are you feeling?"

"I'm okay. Is mom coming today?"

"I don't know, she had to work this morning, but she might be in later this evening."

Charlie looked at his feet under the covers and stretched his toes. A silence drifted through, waiting for a tumbleweed to pass. A faint rush of air could be heard coming from the nasal cannula resting under his nose.

C broke the silence. "But I'm going to be here all day, how does that sound?"

The boy leaned over to not let the doctors in on the top-secret conversation.

"Can we race in the wheelchairs again?" He looked at his dad, eyes now open wide. The corners of his mouth twisted up just a little. Last time they got in trouble when they spun a corner and almost took out a doctor walking a nice old lady with Parkinson's. Even though it was the children's wing, the hospital used it as an overflow area for geriatrics. They all needed the same attention anyway.

C leaned in close and matched his tone. "Just so you know, I'm not gonna let you win this time." The boy laughed. "How about I go get those waffles?"

C got up and made his way around the room. The cabinets were filled with various clothes and blankets. The countertop collected toys and balloons that had been played with and worn. A Lego set of underwater divers and submarines took up the movable table that would otherwise be used for food. Their scuba gear hung on their backs and their respirators attached to futuristic, deep sea helmets. Charlie played with them the most. The idea of being somewhere where *everyone* wore oxygen was enticing. The walls hung pictures of the boy and his parents in happier times. An assemblage of things scattered the room, things brought in over time, left in hopes they would be needed for a long time. C weaved through the various tools for breathing and PT, a gymnasium of equipment and Bots to wait on his every need. For now, they lay dormant and slightly ominous. As C curved around the bed, he accidentally kicked a portable oxygen tank, catching it before it hit the ground. He snapped his head at his son with high eyebrows; Charlie returned the expression and laughed.

* * *

The cafeteria was a jungle. Food and health are the universal common denominators and a hospital cafeteria is where the world meets. Patients, recently in remission, harassing a customer service representative on a phone about how their health care had screwed up, crunching into a piece of toast. Nurses moved in pairs, laughing about the woes of their night shift over their fifth coffee and low-fat cream cheese bagels, kicking the door open with fluorescent clogs. Doctors sat staring at their computers, typing articles and pulling studies, popping cubes of melon and pineapple into their mouths. Administrators chewed on bacon, egg, and cheese sandwiches while telephonically enforcing health care regulations to a customer service representative asking for ammunition. Broken engines, body mechanics, and shop owners breaking bread.

The cafeteria featured a huge array of food stations: grills, a pasta bar, a deli, and stir fry all unfortunately closed until lunch. The only open section was the breakfast line, a reformatting of the salad bar, that offered trays of bagels and muffins, chafers of sausage links and pancakes, bowls of fruit and cottage cheese. A buffet leveled the playing ground, slowly emptying as the line shuffled through. Everyone was a vulture, picking and pulling, assuming that someone somewhere would refill it, never mind the hundred people in line, hungry and waiting. Here, they were all equal.

C stared at the back of the head that stood in front of him. His eyes were sagging. Talking with his son was like coffee, and right now the boost had worn off. The line that droned on in front of him babbled with old ladies talking about the side effects of their beta-blocker medications. Being old was brutal. Stuffing pill after pill, shot after shot into a body that is trying so hard to give up. Holding on to life is so innate and instinctual that all animals strive for it. The problem is that humans have become too good at prolonging it with technology and chemicals. With enough epinephrine, dopamine, and atropine, doctors could get a pulse from a rock. When, instead, they should let the dying die and cling to the memories of what once was, even if it goes against better judgment or forces us to deal with grief. A rotting banana could only be salvaged into banana bread for so long.

When his turn at the food came, he grabbed a banana, spooned out an assortment of cubed fruit, and snagged a cup of yogurt from a pyramid that a Bot had spent the morning running thousands of calculations and algorithms to stack perfectly, and that would inevitably topple when a nice old man with cataracts, who no longer understood physics, wanted a cup from the bottom. Towards the end of the line was a tray of waffles, layered on top of each other. He punched in the number four on a screen and a Bot scooped them out to place on his tray. The lady in line behind him gave a harrumph, assuming he was loading up for himself. He let it go. At the end of the bar was an assortment of toppings, syrup, sugar, and whipped cream. He grabbed two packets of syrup—at some point one had exploded all over the rest of them making the whole basket sticky—and did a quick douse of whipped cream.

There was a juice dispenser on the side of the room. The soda machine next to it was turned off till lunch, a rather passive oppression. C wandered over to it, placed a cup under the apple juice nozzle, and pressed the button. It didn't work. He closed his eyes and took a breath. The face of this perfect place of comfort for yearning masses was crumbling. Hundreds of people before him were sipping at the one thing that made them feel young again, that brought the ease of childhood, cool and refreshing and apple-flavored to their mouths and minds. And now it was gone. *Bastards.* He scooted the cup over and tried for orange juice instead. He pressed the button and a high-pressure stream of water and juice concentrate shot into the bottom of the cup. *If they put a sign that said "Mixed fresh for every cup" they could charge more.* Maybe he should take up marketing. He filled a second cup. The plates were placed on a scale at the cashier and he was charged by weight. It seemed like a lot of money but he was too tired to do the "per ounce" math in his head.

It was easy to forget why he was there or even that he was. His vision was so focused on his son, so enticed by the day-to-day that the big picture seemed unframed and abstract, a canvas that stretched past the horizon. Walking down the hallway brought him back. The beeps and alarms, stethoscopes and scrubs, these things seen in movies that couldn't possibly be real, only images made up in a director's mind of what sick people should look like. He passed room after room, peaking ever so nonchalantly into them. Voyeuristic glances, praying to see person after person who was worse off than he was. It was not schadenfreude, there was no pleasure; it was its own behavior, something that drove him to see the medical misfortune of others with a curiosity of how far life will go, wondering what will be the breaking point. It was a vaccination for death, little bits and pieces creeping into his body, terrified of the whole, trying to get a taste to stow away for later when the disease finally comes.

In the end, we all will lose the battle. We are electric. Currents run through our neurons. Sodium and potassium pumping back and forth, negative to positive and back again. One day, the system will break down, the charges will dissipate, a computer unplugged. There are nothing but elements, atoms that conveniently sit in the right place at the right time and we decide that it's consciousness. There is no discernible difference between the EKG monitor and the person it's connected to. A long list of if/then statements. We are animals who have perfected cause and effect, computers who think that there is a language more sophisticated than binary, but your eyes are either open or closed, your arm is bent or straight, you are either alive or dead. The lottery is always fifty-fifty, either you win or you lose.

C could hear a coughing fit as he approached the room. He hastened his step and swung the corner through the open door, almost tipping the tray as his shoulder hit the door frame. Charlie was sitting up in bed coughing hard, unable to get a full breath in between. A laryngeal spasm, the young PA in residence called it, trying to impress the family, or maybe prove his worth. C slowed, Elizabeth had moved her chair closer to the bed and was holding a hand on Charlie's back. She coached him through it, giving him the moral support that he needed, and soon he was able to settle back down. He laid back in bed, exhausted. Elizabeth looked up at C and smiled worriedly.

"No breakfast for me?," she jested, as she sat back in her chair.

"What are you doing here?"

"My meeting got canceled so I had an hour to kill and my next one is just down the block. Thought I'd drop by to see this little goofball." She looked at Charlie, accusing him of his goofball-ness. He squinted his eyes and smiled.

"Oh, that's great." C sat down, placing the tray of food on the table that hung over the bed.

"Waffles!," Elizabeth yelled, jokingly critical. "You had waffles yesterday!"

Charlie shrunk back his head, swinging his eyes back and forth, chewing on a piece of watermelon.

"You did!" C glared at him. "I thought you hadn't had waffles in 'like a million weeks.'"

"I forgot," he said matter-of-factly as he sat up. He opened a packet of syrup and poured it over his plate. C and Elizabeth looked at each other, trying to figure out how they raised such a conniving son. Charlie dug in.

7 | THE GARAGE

The bruises were healing well. C's face had a yellowish blotch that ran along his left cheekbone, and his nose had a new ridge in the center. He could stand up straight without pain and, as long as he didn't bump into anything, he could pass as good as new. The recovery was a process and his drive to be out and about had suffered. A pizza box sat on the kitchen counter; bowls and glasses littered the coffee table. He was bordering on being a shut-in, the couch, his new Cadillac. It was the pain from the fight, he told himself every hour or so, that kept him stationary. Of course he can't go out, he looked ridiculous, plus everything hurt too much. The meeting with the lawyer crept in and out of his mind. He poked at the bruise on his side, testing it, lingering in the physical pain for a second or two until his mind shifted to something else.

There was a lot of wall staring; the brick wall by the window had become alien to him. *Who laid these bricks? Did they have a machine or did one guy slap on some cement and wedge them in one by one? Who made bricks? They seem to just always be around and always old. Like all bricks were made a thousand years ago and we just recycle them over and over. Where were these bricks before this building? In a grocery store? A prison?* His thoughts spiraled out. The more questions he could ask, the fewer answers he had to find. He thought of the gold line at the bank. *Was it actually gold or just gold paint? Was it just a facade? A flashy show to distract from the cracks in the cement, to repress the idea that the building might be falling apart, that maybe cement wasn't forever, that it, like everything, would come toppling down?* He looked at his TV and sighed.

A vibration came from the ether. A sound like a very rhythm-conscious fly trapped in a screen door. He looked around the couch but couldn't see it. He threw the blanket that he had, at one point, swore would become his personal Shroud of Turin. Still nothing. He jammed his hands in between the cushions, running them back and forth. Frustration was setting in. The vibration ended. He took a deep breath and looked behind him. His phone was sitting on the back of the couch.

One missed call: Sam

He swiped his thumb across the screen, about to call back when a text came through.

> **Sam: Hey buuuddy, Garage in one hour. Take a shower, I'm sure you smell like old Cheetos.**

C tilted his head back against the couch and closed his eyes. He did smell like old Cheetos. He scratched at his head. If he left, then his dreams would fall away and he would have to re-enter the real world and all its pain. If he stayed, he could almost convince himself that the last three years didn't happen and everything would be okay. Another text came through.

> **Sam: Stop debating and get off your couch.**

Sam knew him too well. They had been close friends for over a decade, meeting senior year of college. C worked at a bar that Sam regulared. One night, Sam had lit himself on fire trying to fight some guy who was giving him a hard time. He had created a handheld, pop-out, flamethrower and when some six-foot-six knuckle dragger tried to step up to him, he was over eager to try it out. It didn't go well, but to be fair, once his sleeve was in flames, he was able to pull his arm out and start swinging it like a flaming whip. He managed to drive the guy off with a few singe marks. C put him out with a pitcher of water.

Sam was the go-to when things got rough, and they had. Since graduating from college, Sam had been working as a civil electrician for an electric company. He was in charge of testing gross input/output power to buildings in the city and maintaining transformers. It was an easy job for easy pay. The PII project was C's idea but Sam ended up being a lot of the brains behind the technical aspect. He used his knowledge of the city's electrical grid to cut power to the banks and their alarms and cameras and spent a lot of time studying banking software to find the fastest routes through it. Together they created a brilliant system, and once they brought on other people, Sam, to protect himself and his personal life, went by Tech, which was eventually shortened to T.

C stood up and blood fell from his head, rushing to his feet. He put a hand on the armrest to stabilize himself. His head pounded with his heartbeat for a few seconds and he felt like he was looking through a snowstorm. It passed. He made his way to the kitchen for a drink of water to refill his apparently empty bloodstream. A shower was a good idea. He took his shirt off in the bathroom, stiffly pulling out one arm at a time, and studied the bruising to his ribs. It was healing slower than his face, definitely a fracture. Blue and yellow patches still hugged his side but there was no swelling. The heat of the shower made it feel better. For a long time, he let the water run over his back and down his side. He forgot what it was like to feel things; the shower was a baptism. Hot water drifted from his shoulders to his forehead and back as he swayed gently. It was odd that a little bit of running water could so efficiently bring the dead back to life. *Maybe Jesus was onto something. Maybe there was science behind it.* He threw on jeans and a t-shirt and walked out the door.

* * *

The Garage was a dive bar in the heart of downtown. Decades ago, an old auto body shop was retrofitted to sell booze and tend to the broken. It was furnished with wobbly booths, a pay-per-play pool table (though the payment system had been ripped out and was now free), and a dartboard. Leaned up on top of a half wall, among a collection of old car parts, was a painting of a pregnant woman smoking a cigarette on a couch. An American flag was draped as a blanket over her lap and the coffee table was littered with beer cans and empty cigarette packs. She looked exhausted and beautiful. The bar was smushed between an upscale Italian Gastropub and a clothing store for women who spent too much money wanting other people to think that they didn't care where their clothes came from—the store was called some variation of the word "Bohemian" and the sign was in a font that was not wholly consistent with itself.

The auto shop was built when the city was still a town,

and as the more modern buildings rose up around it, the zoning officials had done all they could to get rid of it. A long series of fire and health and safety inspections later, it still stood defiantly. The owners held on to some old and questionable piece of government signed paper that locked the property tax at a rate meant for early twentieth-century standards. It was framed behind the bar. The facade outside was lightly burned—there was a conspiracy of councilmen trying to burn down the place—and the sign was missing a bulb but, over all, the place had a charm to it.

Inside, a bar ran from the back wall down the right side, turning into an "L" just before the front door to leave an open space for a jukebox and a Hulk-themed pinball machine, which the owner said was "for the kids," though he was caught playing it now and again. Scattered high-top tables with and without bar stools took up the center of the room, booths lined the left side. The whole room was maybe twenty-five feet across but surprisingly deep. A dartboard hung on the far wall and appeared to be the room's center-piece the way the light was focused on it. Neon signs littered the walls advertising various beers and liquors. A "Tin Cup" sign sat in proud display above the front door with a slogan under it that read, "Mountain Whiskey." Patrons loitered and shot the shit, drinking, and yelling, and singing. A group of young veterans got rowdy in the farthest booth, camo hats and tall boots, and arms that used to be able to knock out eighty push-ups in two minutes. Now, they edged on alcoholism and reminisced about the food in towns with Arabic names. Another booth was taken by two ladies who might have shopped at the clothing store next door and decided that this place had "classic bar vibes." They spoke about disrespect and unfairness and sipped at tart and fruity ales—sour beer for sour women. The high tops were taken up by three homeless people who had a good day, and a group of cougars who seductively sucked vodka some-things out of straws while not so casually looking at the vets in the booth. Their push-up bras filled with vicarious daughters and divorced husbands.

C pushed through the door and looked around. Sam was sitting at the bar, talking to the bartender who greeted C as he sat down.

"What happened to you?" The bartender poured a beer.

"He lost a fight." Sam smiled.

C rolled his eyes. "I didn't lose. He got a few good shots."

"Well, as long as you get a few more than they do. This one's on me. You need it more than I do." He set the beer in front of C.

"Thanks, Bob." C touched the glass to his mouth. The carbonation jumped at his nose and the froth nuzzled his lip, a cerveza, limey and refreshing, his favorite. It had been a while since he had a fresh tap beer. There was something about the 16 ounce glass in a bar that changed the flavor. Cans blocked the nose so every beer tasted faintly like the smell of aluminum. When you can bathe in the aroma, feel the fizz on your face, hear the bartender's story about the guy he kicked out the night before, that's a beer. Bob headed down the bar to refill a glass for a guy who may have fallen asleep, empty pint in hand.

"How you been?" Sam turned his focus, quieting his voice.

"I don't know. Last week or so has been tough. We had the meeting with the lawyer. It was hard to keep up appearances."

"What did she say about your face?" Sam drank his beer.

"I told her I got hit by a car. If she asks you, that's the story."

"Damn, dude. Are you gonna try to fight the divorce?"

"I don't know. I signed for a voluntary appearance. I'm kind of regretting it now, but I already made her life miserable. If this is what she wants, then I'm not gonna make it hard for her." C sipped at his beer. He rubbed his forehead with his palm. It was nice to talk it out with someone. So many times he had run it through his head. So many times that it was easy to play both sides and feel bad for himself. Saying it out loud made it real; the words existed in someone else's reality too.

"Ya'll have been through a lot. I don't blame either of you."

C thought about it all. His entire life up until that point. The ups and downs, the bitter lies and tremendous defeats, victories soured by humility, dirtied perfection. He thought about Charlie.

"We need to keep going." C turned to Sam.

Sam looked concerned. "I don't think we can do it with the three of us. Not in the time frame. I mean maybe, but if anything goes sideways we're fucked, and we'll basically be blind the whole time."

"I'll figure something out." The pinball machine started making noise. Two of the vets had made their way over there and were smashing at the paddle buttons. A drunken sloshiness swung their bodies as they laughed, getting overly excited when they hit a bonus, blaming each other for the missed balls. Sitting quietly at the L end of the bar was a kid, maybe twenty-one years old, by himself. He had a drink in front of him, a dark lager, and his arms were crossed resting on the bar. He mostly looked down, occasionally surveying the room with his eyes before returning to his position. C examined him. He wore a white button-down short sleeve shirt and jeans with a green trucker hat pulled down a little far. His left leg was propped up as he balanced the ball of his foot on the crossbar of the stool. Just barely glistening under his pant leg was a silver piece of metal.

"Holy shit." C leaned back in his chair.

"What?" Sam looked around anxiously. C faced forward and sipped his beer.

"That kid over there is Ed's son." C took a swig.

Sam gave him a quick scan. "Ahhh, I forgot he had a kid. He's packin.'"

"I saw. I've seen him around here and there but he mostly keeps to himself. I wanted to reach out but he always had a look about him like he wasn't in the mood. Fuck, I can't remember his name."

"So, what are you thinking?"

"I'm thinking maybe the apple didn't fall far from the tree. Give me a minute." C got up. He strolled over to the jukebox and jabbed at the touch screen. Bob left the jukebox unlocked so anyone could play whatever they wanted for free. "A dollar to play a song? That's some high-quality bullshit," he would say. C flipped through the selection. He threw on an old AC/DC album and turned his attention to the kid at the bar.

"Hey." C sat down next to him.

"What do you want?" The kid furrowed his eyebrows, keeping his eyes straight forward.

"Your father is Ed Arzhen. You grew up in Flatbush." The kid turned his head to study the man who had invaded his afternoon. "I used to live next to you. I was good friends with your dad. You were probably only twelve when I left."

"Yeah. I remember." The kid looked away and took a sip of beer.

"What was your name again? Phil or Bill? I remember the 'ill.'"

"It's Will." He was a bit dismissive.

"Do you remember my name?"

"No."

C nodded and smiled lightly. "Have you heard from your dad recently?"

"No."

"Do you know where he's at?"

"No idea. Jail, dead, I'm not sure." Will looked to be over the conversation. He pulled his beer closer.

"He didn't leave you his number?"

"No."

"Hmm." C thought for a minute. "Are you living downtown?" He walked over to grab his beer while listening for an answer.

"No."

C sat back down next to him. "Yeah, I figured as much. Most people who live over here don't need to be carrying." He said it like he was mentioning the rain that would come later that night.

"What are you talking about?" Will got defensive. He dropped his leg off the stool and tried to casually lengthen his pant leg.

"Hey, man, it's alright. I'm not gonna announce it. Half the people in here are just as hot." Will was on edge, he grabbed his beer trying to flush the rest of it. "Well, if you're carrying that thing around with you I assume you're living out east of 38th. I spent my time on that side of the tracks, I get it. I used to keep a little six-shooter on me too."

Will stopped trying to drown himself. He sat up a bit more and looked at C. He sighed. "It's not loaded, it's just in case I need to flash it at someone. Usually does enough."

"Do you have the rounds on you?"

"Yeah, I have a handful in my pocket." He didn't like that he had been found out.

"Can you shoot?"

He shrugged. "If I have to."

C stared at him for a while; Will looked uncomfortable. He turned his head to his beer and folded his arms again. C looked back at Sam who was talking with Bob. He reached over the counter, hit the feed button on a receipt printer—an old bar with old technology—and grabbed a pen.

"Well, if you need anything, shoot me a message. I might have a way to get you to this side of the tracks." C scribbled on the paper and left it on the table. He threw back the last of his beer and motioned to Sam who did the same. The two left.

* * *

Will stared ahead at the far wall, trying to figure out what had just happened. Who was this guy with the broken face and sketchy life? This odd man bringing up his estranged father? It was somewhere in his memory, he saw fragments, the picture was a jigsaw. He thought about his dad, in jail, in the street, wherever he might be, trying to remember the two of them together. His dad in a gutter and this broken man whose name he couldn't remember. He looked down at the slice of paper. A phone number was scribbled, under which was a single letter. "C."

8 | Phone Calls I

(Three Years Ago)

The phone rang.

C: Hey.

Elizabeth: Hey.

C: How's it going over there?

Elizabeth: It's alright. Charlie is sleeping.

C: Did you talk to the doctor again?

Elizabeth: Yeah.

C: So… What's the move?

Elizabeth: I don't know.

C: Well, what did he say?

Elizabeth: He said the same thing as last time. All they have left is palliative.

C: What about the thing we talked about? Did you bring that up?

Elizabeth: He said it was too experimental and insurance wouldn't cover it. He said the hospital wouldn't even allow it and they would have to call in people from Norway and regardless, the drugs are not approved here.

C: Can we go to Norway?

Elizabeth: I don't know. I don't know the rules about medical flights. In his condition we would probably need a private plane with a nurse to ride with him.

C: I mean they have oxygen condensers on the plane for other sick people. We would get a first-class ticket so he has a bed to lay in, and we hire a nurse to ride on the flight and check on him.

Elizabeth: (Sigh) Can we take out a loan?

C: I don't know. I can try to file for one. Let me look some stuff up. I'll call you later.

* * *

The phone rang.

Elizabeth: Hey.

C: Hi.

Elizabeth: Any luck?

C: No. The airlines I called said there was a liability issue with letting someone as sick as he is on a plane. They recommended an air ambulance. I called around those companies and for a staffed plane to Oslo. It's going to be somewhere around two hundred thousand with the ground transports.

Elizabeth: Two hundred thousand?!

C: I know. That's just for the transport, not even the treatment. I told them the situation and they said it was very unlikely insurance would cover it since it's not being prescribed by a doctor. I filled out the paperwork for a loan but I didn't submit it yet. Are you good with that?

Elizabeth: I don't know. What if it doesn't work? What if we get there and they do all this and it doesn't work? The doctor said it was experimental.

C: So, you're going to give up?

Elizabeth: No, of course not.

C: So, I'll send this loan request in.

Elizabeth: Yeah. Go ahead.

C: Okay. I'll talk to you later.

* * *

The phone rang.

Elizabeth: Hey.

C: Hey.

Elizabeth: What's up?

C: I was thinking.

Elizabeth: About what?

C: Well, I know it's a stretch, but do you think you could get a fundraiser going with the guy who runs your company?

Elizabeth: Umm…

C: I mean I know it's a few steps up but…

Elizabeth: It's *a lot* of steps up. I don't even know how to get in touch with him.

C: Well, I just thought maybe you could set up an appointment or something and try to plead a case. How could he turn down a dying kid?

Elizabeth: I can try to send some emails.

C: Yeah. I mean between him and all his rich friends we could probably raise a good chunk of it. Pitch it as a PR stunt if you have to.

Elizabeth: That might work.

C: It will definitely work. Email them right now.

Elizabeth: Okay. I'll talk to you later.

C: Yes. Definitely. Definitely.

9 | Guards

C kicked his door open at 1:15 a.m. The lights started dimming on slowly. C groaned. "Lights off." The apartment obeyed. He wandered in a stupor through the dark living room, tossing his keys at the counter. They skidded straight across the granite, flew off the other side, and hit the floor. He flopped diagonally into bed face first, sending the cat running for her life. His memory was playing on a loop, trying to figure out which bar he should have called it at. One more came after one more and when it was time to stop, they recounted the events of the past couple weeks and put back another.

There was a softness to his sheets that seemed impossible, the pillows putting light pressure on his bruised ribs was the only thing keeping him awake. The alcohol was winning the battle though. He used his toes to push off his shoes, the thought of ever standing up again was out of the question. Tomorrow was going to be hell. The cat returned to her spot to carefully examine the behemoth that dared disturb her rest and decided he was okay. She sniffed at his nose and curled up on the pillow next to his head. C contorted his body around, never quite comfortable but always very close. It was silent. The faint purr of the cat, the occasional electric hum of a late-night car passing outside the window four stories down. He was enveloped by the clothes he didn't have the energy to take off, the blankets he twisted himself into, the darkness of the room.

Thoughts of the night bounced around his head. At around 9:00, they walked out of Quijano's, a Cuban rum club where old men smoked cigars and ashes littered the floor. They stumbled along down the sidewalk through the city, joking and laughing. A few blocks down they passed a restaurant that C used to frequent. Sitting at a table in the front window was a small group of four women, talking and eating. C tilted his head as he recognized one in the corner as an old friend of Elizabeth's, then another, then finally the fourth woman at the table caught him off guard. C stopped in his place as Sam walked out ahead of him. He stared at her, frozen in time. There she was, just on the other side of the glass. She was laughing, an image that C couldn't recreate in his mind before that point. He wasn't sure if she saw him staring at her through the vinyl lettering on the window. Elizabeth carried on. There was no hint of trauma, of struggle. She sat with elegance and poise, enjoying her night, her dinner. C stood outside and shivered lightly in the wind, a drunken haze twisting around in his head. His mind changed; there was a determination, a mild revenge. *Who was she to make ultimatums?* His head beat slowly. The feeling was short-lived. He tried to hate her, make it easier, but it wouldn't stick. He walked on.

Another bar had an advertisement in the bathroom that featured a picture of a man with a kid on his shoulders. The boy was looking down as the dad looked up. They were laughing, happy. Sun danced on their faces and green trees framed them in the distance. He was maybe six years old, with bleach-blond hair and a toothy smile. The father wore nice clothes. A shiny silver watch glistened in the sun. The bottom of the ad read "Financial freedom, one step away." The True North Bank logo stretched across under it. He fell in a daze looking at the poster and, in the inebriated state he was in, the quick trip to the bathroom suddenly became more dispiriting than he had anticipated.

* * *

The operations had to go on. He wanted a bigger target. More money, smaller hole. But now his crew was short a man. It might be possible. He could take the role, but he had to spend most of his time helping Doc. The surgery had to be perfect every time or they could risk destroying the PII, killing the guy, or worse running out of time. Sam was perfect at his job, he had done so much pre-work that, once everything was plugged in, he mostly just had to run a few programs in sequence. Doc was good, but he was dealing with the live person, out in the open, where anything could go wrong. With no guard, they were exposed. There would be no window checks, no one to keep an eye on the security, very little crowd management. It didn't seem like much, but when everything moves fast, it goes bad fast too.

G came from an old crew before this one. A high-intensity, quick-paced, intimidation type. Their system was less calculated. At first, they held up a single person at the tellers, forcing them at gunpoint to transfer their funds to a joint account that was then uploaded to the Angiocoin bank. One guy ran the transfers while the other two kept watch, but when they realized the rich generally don't keep much uninvested cash in their accounts, they started doing three at a time. One shooter per target per teller, trying to rush it and no longer checking their backs. The allure of a bigger score per person motivated them, invincible to the civilian world, or so they thought. All it took was a James Billmen with a 9mm in his waist and the preoccupied minds of the guys with the guns. One crew member and two civilians were killed. G narrowly made it away. Ed was friends with the other guy in G's gang that survived and connected with G by proxy.

Quickly, C found that G's paranoia was difficult to manage. The way his old crew ended left him on edge and trigger happy, always observant to a fault. He regularly looked over his shoulder, recorded all his calls, his house was filled to the brim with cameras and microphones that he checked almost hourly. He fell into a drug habit, thinking that the stimulants he took were giving him elevated senses. He only trusted himself.

The whole story scared the hell out of C, and for a cautious man it was enough to never leave the public unattended. Carrying a gun was becoming less uncommon, and if there wasn't someone with a keen eye on it, there could be trouble. Sometimes, there are too many heroes in the world. C knew they needed another man, nothing would happen until they had him.

C rolled over on his bed and stared at the ceiling. It spun slowly. Images of Elizabeth and G flashed on the backs of his eyelids, their faces passing each other in a flurry of lights. Nausea crept in and out like a tide and his breathing matched the current.

C slipped quietly into a dream of Charlie playing in the backyard, shovel in hand, dirt on face. He was, as always, looking for dinosaur bones that might have been left behind just under the mulch. In the dream, he found one. The brown fossil presented itself up through the garden. C couldn't understand why he never noticed the three-foot-tall skull sticking up out of the flower bed, but Charlie ran to it, digging at its base, deeper and deeper until a thirty-foot by thirty-foot hole outlined a full Tyrannosaurus Rex skeleton. And then Charlie crawled up out of the hole, but he was older. An adult with a child's face. Excitement gleamed in his eyes. It started to rain slowly, then harder. In the distance, two men fought in a parking lot. Charlie looked back to the dinosaur bones in disappointment. As the water touched the fossil, the bones began to melt. Charlie cried out, now a kid again. C looked around desperately. A tarp hung over the side of the house where renovations were being done. He ran to it and pulled, but it didn't come down. He pulled and pulled but it would not release. He ran up the stairs which rotted away as he stepped on them. At the top of the house he could hear the rain beating down on the tarp. Charlie cried louder. C grabbed a knife from a bucket and cut the tarp loose. It whipped in the rain and shot down off the house, dragging him with it. He grabbed a gutter rail. The tarp twisted around his leg pulling him with the wind. Below him, a thousand feet down, the dinosaur evaporated slowly. Above, the water pooled in the now exposed house, flooding the bedrooms, the hallways. Charlie went silent, staring into the pit where the bones dissolved in the acid rain. C called to him but he couldn't hear. Charlie took a step towards the edge of the pit. C screamed louder and louder, his throat searing. The house started to overflow with water and the gutters ran with rapids. His hands started slipping. He checked below him. Charlie stepped forward again, leaning out over the melting skeleton. C swiveled his head back and forth yelling. Finally, far down below him, Charlie stepped off, into the pit, sinking down with the bones. C cried. His heart beat through his chest. Another gust of wind took the tarp out, pulling his ankle like a sail. He was ripped from the house and fell.

C shot up in bed. His face was layered with sweat and his head spiraled. He leaned over the edge of the mattress and vomited on the floor. There was silence in the room. The cat had relocated to avoid the stirring. Outside, thunder struck quietly in the distance and a light rain teetered off. The smell of a heavy storm permeated the cracks in the walls. C reached for his phone to check the time. He had a message.

Unknown: Where can we talk?

10 | INTRODUCTIONS

The room smelt of stale beer and bad air freshener. If the orange couch was ever washed by the original owners who dropped it on the side of the road, then that was the last time it was. The unit was supposed to just be a fall-back location, a rallying point to get heads straight and to store gear, but one day they walked in and Sam had single-handedly dragged the couch in there, beginning the transformation from bare-bones headquarters to a shaggy man cave. It was followed by a TV, a mini-fridge, and a pool table in the bay. Even a zombie pinball machine lit up the corner of the office. C had been against the whole thing, straining to keep the job professional, but he was outvoted and eventually gave in.

He pretended to be disappointed, but truly anything to get him out of his house at the time was welcomed. Posters had found themselves tacked to the walls. Pinups and beer advertisements, Sam liked the feel of a secret planning room and he had seen a few too many Tarantino films. Whatever keeps them motivated was C's stance. He just wanted his cut, but if someone needed to lose in billiards, he would roll his eyes and say, "Alright, I'll play ya ONE," which was never the case. It was a good distraction. Sometimes he thought Sam had orchestrated the whole thing for him, to keep his mind occupied. C often caught him watching from a distance, making sure he was happy, at least in that moment. He was a good friend, a trash pool player, but a good friend.

C sat at the table and stared at the safe. It was monolithic, really far bigger than what they needed but he liked the organization it allowed. He looked at his watch, 2:47 pm ticked along. Car tires stuttered over the broken concrete outside the door. C got up and walked to the blind-covered window. He split the plastic bars and watched the brake lights on an old gray sedan turn off. The door opened and a black-booted foot stepped out. The kid was taller than C thought. He had seen him sitting at the bar, but now standing upright in the parking lot he could see Will was long and lanky like his mom. C dropped the blinds and took a step back. He looked around the room, reviewing how much information he was going to tell this kid. If he was anything like his dad then they would be set. Ed was a wild card in the best way. He knew the limit and pushed it with finesse, never going too far, but always going far enough. C wondered where he was. Hopefully, his son was the next best thing.

* * *

Will knocked on the door. He heard a series of locks twist and click and finally the door swung open.

"You're late."

"Sorry, I got lost."

C opened the door all the way and gestured to the table. Will shuffled inside, looking around suspiciously, eyeing the large gun safe with caution. He sat at the table as his eyes adjusted to the room from the sun. The place looked like the 1990s threw up a bachelor pad in a mechanic shop. The gun safe was concerning.

He didn't get lost on the way there. He had turned around twice, talking himself in and out of it, and walking into this place he still couldn't put a finger on what he had gotten himself into. There was something off about the secrecy. He was not a criminal. Sure he smuggled an extra sandwich from a chain convenience store every once in a while, but work had been nonexistent since the autonomous revolution took full swing. He would be happy mopping floors or flipping burgers but why pay some kid the $23 minimum wage when they could get a Bot that pays itself off. The best thing he could do was find the odd job, but it never lasted. He wanted to get out of the east side. His father promised they would, but all these years later, same apartment, same income, no father.

"Why are you here?" C was sitting on the opposite side of the table. His hands were folded and the light above made him look yellow.

Will snapped out of his train of thought. "Um… I… I need money."

"We all need money. Why are you *here*."

"You asked me to come." He was confused. C rubbed his eye and shook his head.

"Alright, I need you to understand something. This is not a regular job. It requires absolute commitment. There is no bailing, no 'oh, I got a thing.' What I will tell you might as well be CIA top-secret shit as far as you're concerned. Do you understand that?"

Will stirred in his chair. "Ye… Yeah."

"You are here solely because you share DNA with a good man. You are here on his behalf. I understand you had a rough time with him growing up, and maybe you don't even know him, or care to, but his reputation and his legacy are the reason you are being given this opportunity. Don't fuck it up." C's eye contact was solid, strong, demanding.

"I understand. I'm sorry." Will retreated.

C took a beat. "I know Ed struggled with the parenting thing, but I promise he meant well. You probably didn't see it much, but he felt bad he couldn't do more for you. He was very determined in the other things he did which made him an expert in his job."

"Tech support?"

"No, his other job."

Will squinted his eyes.

"I don't understand."

"Your dad and I worked together in a not-so-legal sense before he disappeared. A small operation that brought in a little supplemental income. He was good." C sat back in his chair. "Once he left, I started thinking, and that led to the operation I have now. Here. I have an opening and would like to bring you on, but like I said, it's full commit-ment. You have to want it."

Will swallowed. He didn't know about his dad's side dealings, he just thought he used the garage for extra work space from his mechanical job. He knew this was going to be something illegal. He was starting to remember C more and more as he talked, trying to pin down his name. The more he thought about it, the more he recounted; his dad only ever called him C. He came by their house now and again to pick up his dad or to hang out in the garage. Will was never allowed to be in there while C was around. It made more sense now. Ed was okay for most of his life. Will could tell that he wasn't cut out for fatherhood, but he attended school events and cheered him on. He forgot things a lot and didn't seem to really know how to raise a child as far as discipline or even what to feed it, but he looked like he wanted to do well and that's what mattered. His mom took care of him the most, but she worked more than Ed did.

It was towards the end, when Will was fourteen or fifteen and going through the normal rage of puberty, that Ed started disappearing for days on end. He cared less, drank more. He was angry a lot and couldn't keep it together. A rather unfortunate altercation took place in front of Will's school one day that got Ed arrested. He had been gone for just over three weeks and on the upswing decided to surprise Will after school. Another dad made a comment about him smelling like booze and Ed lost it. Will walked out to see his dad being escorted away by police. As the car pulled away they made eye contact. Ed's eyes hung, he managed a small smile and took a deep breath. He mouthed the words "I'm sorry." That was the last time Will saw his father.

Now sitting in this dingy office/lounge thing, he didn't know what to do. He thought about his life at home. His mother, now struggling as a nurse in an industry that was overrun with automatic monitor hookups and medication dispensers. A doctor with a few buttons had taken most of her job description. He thought about the apartment his father left them, six hundred square feet, tucked away on a street where the sun didn't shine well and windows were shuttered after 8:00 pm. He thought about his daily grind, trying to find a job, a gig, anything to get paid, so he could help his mom pay rent and put dinner on the table. It was agony. Some rich guy once said that money doesn't buy happiness. That pissed him off.

Everyone has a line. A "how far are you willing to go" line. Will stared at the table and tried to find his. He knew that he could do petty crimes, as long as they targeted the top percent. They could afford the loss. The government had tried to redistribute wealth a dozen times, but too many tried to work the system and it always collapsed when the people got greedy. When it comes to handouts, there are always a few that start biting the hand. In the end, there were the rich and the poor. The people who designed the machines, and the people who built them. It had to be worth it. He hesitated in his answer

"Um…"

"Come with me."

They walked out to the bay where there were tools and workshop equipment scattered around. If it was used, it hadn't been for a while. On the right side of the garage was a massive metal shell with a white van sitting next to it. The metal box looked like a box truck from the outside, though the frame sat on jack stands instead of wheels and the cargo door swung up and out instead of retracting in.

"Whoa."

Will moved around inside the hull. The top was lined with large metal clamps with wiring that ran along the edges. He dragged his hand along the small rubber bumpers that studded the inside.

"What is this thing?"

"This is the car cover."

He stood in the empty cab and knocked on the glass of the windshield.

"But, how…?"

"The van pulls under it and those clamps grab the roof

JACKSON REZEN

rack. Then hydraulics push the whole body off the ground and the back closes like an old garage. At a glance from the outside, it looks like a regular truck."

Will continued to inspect the machine, speaking without looking up. "Why?"

"Makes a cleaner getaway. If the police are looking for a van, they aren't looking for a truck. Simple."

"Why don't you just pull the van into the back of a truck? Like in the movies."

"Because that involves a much bigger truck and someone to get out and switch vehicles. With this," C tapped the side, the metal rang, "we can pull in, lift it up, and keep driving in five seconds."

"So you do robberies." Will had deduced quickly though saying it out loud he sounded slow.

"Yes, we do." C walked away from the cover towards the tools where he leaned against the work table and crossed his arms. Silence.

"Your father built most of this thing."

Will was pushing a clamp that closed as it recessed.

"What?" Will looked over his shoulder. His hand froze. His world imploded. "I thought you said he disappeared."

"He did. He resurfaced for a couple weeks a few years later when this project was being built. He was going to join us, but right when we finished he told me he had to leave. This was his project. The fastest way to do a vehicle switch without an extra person and without leaving a car behind. We worked on it for three weeks straight but he was the one here night and day figuring out the hydraulics and mechanisms. Like I said, he was incredible."

Will took a deep breath and bit his lip. He looked around the machine again. The last relic of his estranged father. He could imagine him hammering away at tin in this shop, screwing in bolts, cutting, welding, building. His hands touched every part of this box. Even with the slow dilapidation of his father's image wedged in his mind, the small memories of support and dedication peered through, chipping away at it. Will closed his eyes and smiled.

"If you join us, this thing would be part of your job description." C approached Will who stared at the roof. This incredible machine, somehow passed to him by his father. It felt religious. "So, are you in?" Will took another deep breath and nodded. A satisfying nod with only the smallest bit of fear creeping through his eyes. C offered his hand.

"Yeah, I'm in." Will grabbed it firmly with one last look around the shell.

"Good. 'Cause if you changed your mind I'd have to kill you." C laughed. Will did so too, nervously.

11 | Phone Calls II

(Three Years Ago)

The phone rang.

C: Hey.

Elizabeth: Hey.

C: Did you hear back?

Elizabeth: (Silence)

C: What? What was it?

Elizabeth: I just got the email. He ran it through the board and they didn't feel it was appropriate.

C: What!? What do they mean, not appropriate?

Elizabeth: Hold on, I'll read it.

(Typing)

Elizabeth: "After much consideration, the board members and I have decided that it would be inappropriate to offer financial assistance at this time. We feel that to provide a donation to you would create dissonance among the company and lead to other employees asking for handouts. I personally would like to express my condolences on behalf of everyone here for your situation and will keep your daughter in our thoughts and prayers."

C: DAUGHTER!?

Elizabeth: I don't know.

C: Did he even listen to you in the meeting!?

Elizabeth: I thought so. He seemed very genuine.

C: Of course he did. He's a fuckin' schmoozer. He can't even listen 'cause he's too busy trying to look the part. What a fuckin' asshole.

Elizabeth: I know.

C: Did he use the word handouts?

Elizabeth: Yeah.

C: Our son is dying! It's a drop in the bucket for these pricks. They can't offer up a fuckin' comparable penny for a dying kid?

Elizabeth: I tried to email him back but it was sent from one of those no reply emails.

C: This is the fuckin' problem. These rich cocksuckers bop around from their yachts to their planes and can't spare a dime for the people around them.

Elizabeth: Honey, I don't... I don't know what to do.

C: We'll do it ourselves. We don't need some arrogant prick's money.

Elizabeth: How?

C: I'll do it. I'll figure it out.

* * *

The phone rang.

C: Hey.

Elizabeth: Hey.

C: What's up?

Elizabeth: Have you checked the page today?

C: Yeah, my cousin and his wife donated five hundred dollars.

Elizabeth: That's so nice of them. I'll write them a note.

C: Yeah, very nice.

Elizabeth: Did you see the family a couple houses down gave a hundred?

C: No, which ones?

Elizabeth: I know it's horrible but I can't remember their names. Their kid's name is Bastian.

C: Ethan and Sandra.

Elizabeth: Yes, that's right.

C: (Silence)

Elizabeth: We're getting there.

C: (Silence)

Elizabeth: Did you hear back from the loan appeal.

C: No.

Elizabeth: I'm glad we at least got the seventy-five thousand.

C: (Silence)

Elizabeth: How's Charlie doing?

C: He's okay. Do you want to talk to him?

Elizabeth: Sure!

Charlie: Hi mom.

Elizabeth: Hey, honey! How are you feeling?

Charlie: I'm okay.

Elizabeth: That's good, sweetie.

Charlie: Are you (breath) coming today?

Elizabeth: No, not today, I will be there first thing tomorrow though. Daddy is going to stay there till you fall asleep.

Charlie: Okay.

Elizabeth: I'll be there when you wake up, okay?

Charlie: Okay, mom.

Elizabeth: I love you.

Charlie: I love you too.

(Phone rustling)

C: I'll check in with you tonight.

Elizabeth: Okay. I'll talk to you then.

Elizabeth: Hey.

C: Yeah?

Elizabeth: We'll get the money. Don't worry.

C: I'm working on it.

12 | Baby Steps

"Welcome back." C opened the door to the lounge to let Will in. Doc was flipping through a textbook at the table while T played pinball in the corner. They both snapped their head up to the new face coming into their secret lair.

"Well, well, well." T left his game and reached a hand out. "I saw you at the bar but I don't believe we met." Will shook his hand pensively.

"Hi, I'm…"

"Shhhhh, shhhh, shush." T smushed his finger to Will's mouth. "No names."

"…Okay," Will mumbled as T held his lips closed.

T smiled and turned around to the table. "You will know me as T, short for Tech, and this is Doc, short for Doc." He gestured to Doc as he sat at the table. "Come take a seat." Will obeyed.

"Nice to meet you." Doc offered his hand. Will shook it.

C started, "Personal information is prohibited here. From now on, your name here will be G. It is short for Guard. Everyone will call you G. You will not tell them your name, who you are, where you are from, where you live, what you do for work, and you will not ask the same of anyone else. Understand?"

Will nodded. His eyes shifted a little, mulling over an inkling.

"As you know, you can address me as C which is short for Captain. Any questions?"

Will shook his head.

"Great, let's get to it." C walked to the safe and punched in a code that Will could not see. He pulled the door open. "What do you know about the PII?"

Will looked at his wrist where his own implant sat. A soft orange glow tinted his skin above it.

"The Personal Identification Implant," Will said as if reading from a user manual. "I don't know. It has all my information on it."

"What kind of information?" C was pulling things out of the safe and laying them on the table.

"Like my bank, my license and passport, records." C was reaching into the safe and stopped moving for a second on the last word.

"Do you know how it works?," he continued.

"I know it uses blood, right? Transfers everything magnetically, I need a gesture PIN to access it. That's about it."

C finished and turned to face Will.

"And what happens if you take it out?"

Will furrowed his eyebrows. "You can't."

"Well, you can't. But if someone were to hold you down and cut open your wrist and take it out of you, what would happen?"

Will's eyes widened. He was right. He had followed the stories. The guys that went around cutting out people's PIIs. It was the biggest sensation since Jesus. They had news reporters and groupies and conspiracy nuts following their every move. It was mania. People wore their shirts. Riots against the rich had sported their masks and people chanted their name. In a world where the rich were pharaohs and the poor revolted, they were the most famous bank robbers in history. But, they were a mystery. They were always gone before the cops showed up and left a lot of blood and a doped-up man lying on a table with a scar on his wrist and no PII. This was the guy. This was their headquarters. He was being invited into the most sought-after criminal crew and was sitting in their home base with their leader.

"You're the Cut Wrist Crew." It was a name the media had given them. C thought it had a nice ring to it. Will looked around the room at the other two. Doc gave a light smile and T waved his hands like a magician after he pulled out the rabbit.

"Yes." C sat down.

"Oh my god, you just robbed True North last month."

"Well, we didn't rob the bank, we robbed a 46-year-old half-a-billionaire investor in the last oil dynasty in the country named Michael Stutsman."

"Yeah, yeah, right. But I don't understand. How do you…" He trailed off when he realized C was staring at him disapprovingly. "Sorry. You guys are a big deal."

"You're damn right." T dropped a fist on the table. C shot him a glare.

"I know. And now that you know who we are, you are committed. You will not speak to the police, the media, your mother, your friends, anyone about us, about this place, about anything. Is that understood?" C had taken on an aggressive front. He spoke his words clearly and exactly and looked Will in the eye while he did it.

"Yes. I understand."

Will nodded. C reached down and picked up the black box with the clear top. The display was off and the clear part had a light reddish tint to it. He held it up in front of Will.

"This box is the key." He set it on the table. Will looked at it with amazement. He picked it up and flipped it around in his hands.

C continued, "The PII has a series of safeguards built into it. It was designed so that idiots don't go around cutting people's wrists open or digging up graves trying to get their device and pull the information. You're right, it's powered by a chemical reaction between electrolytes in the blood. If you remove that flow of electricity then it will shut off and erase its own data. Once that happens it needs to be brought to a certified insertion facility and they can pull a backup and re-download which is a whole process and requires a lot of identification and is guarded like Fort Knox. As a secondary security measure, the device also needs a constant electric pulse. It sends a signal up the vein which needs to get a reply from an electric beat in the heart. If there is no pulse for more than fifteen seconds, the device locks, more than a minute, same thing, the device shuts down and formats."

Will shifted back and forth between the device in his hand and the man who seemed to know everything about this thing in his wrist. The PII had been around for about ten years and it had spread quickly after its release. New versions had come out and updates were made but people like Will only had the base model that came out early and was not as fancy as the new ones. They were advertised as extremely secure but the average person didn't know the details of how they worked, just how to use them.

"So this thing…" Will looked at C and held up the box.

"This is the charger." C took the device from Will. He flipped a switch on the bottom and the screen flashed. The number seventy appeared with a flashing dot underneath. He flipped open the lid. "This gets filled with the target's blood and a small electrode gives off a series of signals to mimic a heartbeat. It's beating right now at seventy beats per minute, an average heart rate. During the job, we can change it up to match the heart rate of the patient. We are not sure if a drastic reduction in signal from a stressed-out one hundred-fifty to a calm seventy has any impact on the device, so we try to dwindle it down every few minutes. As you can assume, there's not a lot of research on PII removal."

C flipped the device off and placed it on the table.

"Wait, so where did you get that?"

"I designed it." T jumped into the conversation. He was chewing on gummy peaches though Will could not figure out where he was pulling them from. "It's probably the greatest invention of our generation." T stretched his back as he spoke. He leaned forward and picked it up. "3D printed the outside, the wiring is modified from a strobe light but sends an electrical signal the same voltage as the sinoatrial node produces in the heart to the PII."

C picked up the black roll of fabric and spread it over the table. A small collection of shiny surgical tools sat in pockets: a scalpel, two pairs of forceps, a syringe and needle, and a small vial. Will caught the glare from the corner of his eye and quickly seemed uncomfortable, adjusting himself further back in the chair. C picked up the scalpel.

"The tricky part is the extrication." He inspected the sharpness of the blade and placed it back in the pocket. "Doc here does the surgery."

"It's a pretty simple procedure." Doc spoke up for the first time. "We throw a tourniquet on to stop the blood flow. Makes things less messy. Then the wrist gets cut right above the device." He spun the tools around to face him and pointed to each as he described their use. "Then I take these two forceps," he picked them up and snipped the air, "and pinch off the vein that the PII is attached to. Again, that cuts down on the amount of lost blood. The PII is actually only about the size of a grain of rice so it sits right in the wall of the vein with the bottom half resting in the blood flow. I cut that section and pull the thing out with tweezers." Doc rolled the instruments back up. "Like I said, simple." Doc smiled. "This is the fun stuff." He lifted from his chair and reached across the table to pick up the vial. "This is ketamine. Analgesic and dissociative. It takes the pain away and conveniently makes them forget what happened. Sort of chemically zoning out. I mix it with some fentanyl which together gives them a good little ride."

"So you get them high, cut open the wrist, pull out the PII, and then what? Shouldn't they just bleed out?" C picked up what looked like a taser with a small rod at the end. He pressed a button on the side and a blue spark danced on the tip. It buzzed loudly. Will jumped in his seat at the noise.

"Military-grade cauterizer." C raised his eyebrows as if to say, "Impressed?"

Doc jumped in, "They use them in the Army for quick

hemorrhage control in place of tourniquets so people can get back to the fight quicker. It hurts like all hell but it's better than being dead." C put down the cauterizer and proceeded to talk about the rest of the equipment.

"This is a generator with the Wi-Fi transmitter built in to start the computer back up after T cuts the power. It also is the main terminal that everything plugs into. You don't need to worry about it." He pulled an elastic band onto his forearm. "This is cool." It was black with eight small one-by-one-inch boxes attached around it. "This is a gesture tracker." He took it off and handed it to Will. "They invented them as a sort of remote for computers but when that didn't catch on the company pivoted the technology to smart prosthetics. It tracks the electrical signals your muscles send when you move your hand. It's the same concept as your PIN."

Sam jumped in, mouth full of gummies. "I modified it to record and play back the signal." Will was entranced. He moved his hand around and gestured out his PIN, watching the muscles in his forearm move. Though the term PIN didn't really fit in context since it was a hand movement and not a number, the name stuck around. Fear of change and all.

"What are those?" Will pointed to the two metal sheets in the back of the safe. C grabbed one and dragged it out. It scraped the ground with a high note.

"Yes. These are Psych Locks. They use them in psychiatric wards to hold someone down quickly. You just hit them with this middle part. T stand up."

"Ugh, come on man, make Doc do it."

"Nope, all you."

T stood up reluctantly with a pout and placed his arms

along his sides. He tensed his whole body. C swung the metal sheet at his torso where it violently snapped and curled around T's body. He let out a grunt and the rest of the breath he was holding.

"The best part is as they struggle, it tightens down."

"Holy shit!" Will's eyes were wide. "That looks like it hurts quite a bit."

"It's not too bad. The foam rubber on the inside softens a lot of the impact."

"Yeah, okay." T shot back aggressively. "You do it next time."

"It's not the most fun. Give me a hand." T leaned his chest against the door frame to give them leverage. C grabbed one end of the sheet and nodded to Will to grab the other side. They started to pull and Will quickly realized it would take more strength than he thought it should. C grunted. "In the hospital they have a device that opens these but it's bulky." The Psych Lock disagreeingly straightened out and finally snapped back into the long rigid board that it started as. T shook out his arms and rubbed his chest where the metal struck.

C opened a box on the floor of the safe and pulled out an old flip phone. He turned it on, the screen flashed and a brand logo danced. He tossed it to Will who caught it awkwardly.

"This is our communication. Keep it extremely secure. There is no GPS, no internet. It receives texts and phone calls. It remains off when not in use. You will check it at 9:00 pm every night for updates." His speech seemed rehearsed. "If we have a job scheduled you will check it more regularly, but we will get to that when it comes. There is a weird echo around this building on the phone. I think there is a radio tower somewhere a few blocks over. If you need to come to this building send me a message so I can unlock the door remotely. There are cameras around the whole building that I monitor daily so you are welcome to come here, it looks good to the surrounding units to have people back and forth, but no one else can know this place exists. As far as anyone knows, we are a box truck servicing company. I'll give you a script to memorize if people ask."

C placed the equipment back in the safe and grabbed a handgun off a bracket on the back wall, complete with a Bond-style silencer.

"This is your tool." He cleared the weapon and handed it over to Will. "Are you ready?"

"Ready for what?"

"To learn to do the job you were brought here for."

Will had almost forgotten he was here for work and not just a private tour of the world-famous crew's operations.

"Oh... Yes."

"Come on."

In the bay, tools were pushed aside and the van was moved under the cover. With a few carefully placed tables, the open side of the garage was transformed into a mock bank.

"Alright, this is very simple. A lot of things are going to happen around you but the most important thing is that you are focused solely on the crowd. The customers and the staff. That is your only job."

Will nodded.

"The gun will be loaded but you will not shoot it." C moved in closer. "This weapon is almost exclusively for scare tactics, do you understand?" Will could smell his breath.

"Yes."

"The only time you will ever fire this will be if there is another person with a gun who is actively pointing it at you or one of us. Otherwise, wave it around, bang it on the table, do whatever you need to keep order." C stepped back. "Great. Any questions?"

Will turned the gun around in his hands, feeling the weight and the grain. "No. I don't think so."

"Good." C motioned for T to stand in the middle. "Here's the process. We are all going to move in at the same time." C's hand went up. "Oh shit, I almost forgot." He hustled to the lounge and came back with a closed sign and a small sheet of wood with a handle screwed to the bottom. "This is the closed sign. Once we walk in, you are going to slap this sign on the window. It's not foolproof but it works as a mild deterrent just in case. For passersby. The wood you place between the magnetic locks at the top of the outside door. Keeps us from getting trapped in the vestibule. The power should stay off so they wouldn't be able to lock it anyway but this is just a manual backup. If all else fails, we need to at least get out." C went back to where the entrance of the bank would be. "Okay, so we all move in." They started moving forward towards T. "You will announce to everyone that they are to kneel on the ground facing the wall with their hands above their head. Do that now."

Will had been studying their movements and was partially lost in thought trying to figure out what he had gotten himself into. He took a moment to realize that C was talking to him. "Oh…uh." He regained composure. "Everybody on the ground, face the wall, hands on your head." It was pathetic.

105

"No, no, no. It's an order, you need to instill the fear, the hesitation from the start. Be loud, be aggressive. Again."

Will took half a breath and started again. "Everyone!," he croaked, "get down on the ground right now…"

"Point the gun. Finger off the trigger."

Will obeyed. "Get down on the ground and face the wall. Put your hands on your head!" He felt like an idiot yelling at the corner of the empty room.

"Better. We'll work on it."

The four of them ran through the choreography step by step, job by job. Everything was explained in detail from the time structure to troubleshooting. They played out scenario after scenario. What if the target refuses to give the PIN? What if they pass out? What if the bank staff causes problems? What to do with security guards? Information piled on top of information. Will did his best to organize it all but he was awkward in his delivery. C was sure the adrenaline of the actual thing would spark him but there was a mild concern that he made the wrong call. The only way to find out was to do it live.

After a week of running every possible outcome C had laid out, they called it a day.

"Go home, digest. Think of more problems that could arise and what you can do to stifle them." C started packing gear up. "Tomorrow you will come back and we will replay some of these in the dark with the headlamps."

"In the dark?"

"The lights go out, remember. It's not too bad, the windows let in a lot. But there are always corners. Then we do driver training."

"Driver training?"

"Yeah, remember what I said, that cover is your responsibility now. You are the driver." Will's eyes were wide and a mild sweat dewed on his forehead. "You'll be fine. We'll practice."

13 | The Psych Wing

(Three years ago)

C found himself in the wrong part of the hospital. Charlie was in the emergency department again and C had been sitting with him for the last few hours waiting for chest X-rays and bloodwork to come back. He wandered out of the room in search of a bathroom and was directed down a hallway, through the maze of room after room. Some had curtains drawn, others open wide, their residents on display. The disparity was incredible. In some rooms, patients scrolled their phones. They may have been there for a little nausea or mild anxiety, but would cure up with time and a couple of placebos.

In other rooms, people's bodies clung to life without their consent. These were the interesting ones. C paused for a brief moment at one of them. Blood-splattered sheets wrapped around a man almost the size of the bed. The array of blankets and sheer size of the body made it difficult to discern where he ended and the mattress began. An uncountable number of monitors beeped and flashed around him, measuring every movement, twitch, and beat. He lay there, unconscious and alone, probably unaware that he was not in his bed at home. The wires and tubes that crossed him twisted in a rat's nest on his large, round belly, and cascaded off. Some ran up along his sides and tangled themselves in cord organizers before ending in medication pumps. Others fell to the floor and then swung out to a monitor far behind his head with a huge display of his blood pressure, heart rhythms, and ten other measurements that C could only guess at. A large tube snaked its way over his face and down his throat. The other side plugged into a wheeled machine with a squeeze pump pushing up and down. His chest matched the inverse of the pump. This man existed only as a beating heart and even that would crash if not for the drugs. C thought back to Charlie. He was so small in his bed compared to this man, so delicate. If the doctors could keep this medical disaster alive, surely they could bring Charlie around.

C carried on down the corridor dodging EMS stretchers and scribes who typed away as they walked. The yelling started as he turned the corner. At the end of the hallway was a large group of security officers and a handful of nurses, horse-shoeing around the opening to a room with floor to ceiling glass doors. C moved closer slowly. In the room a six foot three, two hundred and thirty pound man was conveying his disapproval of the staff. According to his protests, the staff had done nothing to track down the man that was controlling his brain from an apartment two miles away. At the nurses' station, someone was drawing up a series of medications. C passed another security officer watching another room. He was overweight, with glazed-over eyes, and generally uninterested in the fireworks next door.

"What's going on in there?"

"Welcome to the psychiatric wing."

"Ahh."

"Are you looking for someone?"

"Well, no, I was trying to find the bathroom and I think I made a wrong turn."

"Oh, yeah, there is one back that way to the left." The officer gestured lazily.

C looked back the way he came and saw the turn he missed. He nodded to the nurses' station. "What are they going to do?"

"B52."

"What?"

"Benadryl, five milligrams of Haldol, two milligrams of Ativan. Knocks 'em right out. Standard for schizophrenic breaks."

"Damn. They got a blow dart?"

"Oh, no. They have Psych Locks."

"What?"

The officer pointed at a large male nurse carrying two metal sheets. They were around five feet long and a foot and half wide with what looked like foam rubber on one side. "Psych Locks. They swing 'em into the patient and they curl around him like a spring."

"Like they hit him with it?"

"Sort of, doesn't take much force. You're not supposed to be wandering around, you know, HIPPA and everything, but if you mosey on that way in about thirty seconds you'll seem 'em go. Don't go hanging around too long though."

C nodded slowly, keeping his eyes on the room. "Thanks." He walked casually around the nurses' station to get a better view, keeping his distance. Over the shoulders of the staff he could see the male nurse with one Lock and a large security officer with the other. The door to the room was pulled open on a count of three and the two men shuffled in. The patient tried to turn and run to the corner of the room but the nurse was quick and slapped the first lock around his chest with a loud snap. C flinched at the noise that rang throughout the emergency department. The other was quickly snapped around the patient's legs and as he tumbled the nurse directed him towards the bed. The other staff flooded the room. The B52 was administered and everyone left. The patient laid there wriggling on the bed waiting for the drugs to kick in, cursing loudly, and generally feeling sorry for himself.

14 | DRIVE

The next few days were full of driver training. They talked through placement and how to set themselves up for success by finding the exact right location to hide the cover that was both concealed and quickly accessible. Combing the area was a big part of G's job. C set up a projector in the lounge.

"So you can get an idea." He had a satellite map of the surrounding area with small blue dots clustered through the city. He pointed at a red dot in the upper right corner. "This is us." His finger slid down to the left. "Over here are the past targets we've hit." To the southwest around seventy miles away was an amalgamation of twelve blue dots. "As you can see, G, we keep our business a good distance from us and in the same direction so we can't be triangulated. That means we have to drive pretty far with the cover on to make it there and back and there can't be any hiccups or stops along the way. It is extremely important to maintain your speed, your signals, your merging. We cannot get pulled over. Ever." C looked Will in the eyes. "Understand?"

"Ye...yes." Will nodded.

"Before every job, we will do a full vehicle inspection. Make sure everything is pristine and is not going to break down or get us pulled over. Things like the oil, the van lights, the connector for the truck lights, all need to get checked."

"What connector?"

"The cover has a contact point in the false cab that lines up with a magnetic point on the van's grill and powers the headlights and taillights on the truck body."

"Whoa."

"Yes, and that all needs to be tested rigorously before we do anything." C returned to the map and indicated the green dots scattered around the blue ones. "These are the previous spots where we placed the cover. As you can see they are generally in industrial zones, under overpasses, or by junkyards. We can reuse some if it's the obvious choice but always be on the lookout for something better." C's eyes were fixed on the map.

* * *

For the driving training itself, C had set up four cones topped with poles and wrapped in a tarp horseshoe that was barely bigger than the van. Will had to pull into it so perfectly that he could do it every time without fail in the light, the dark, at a three-mile-per-hour approach up to a twenty-mile-per-hour approach. This they could do on the weekends in the lot and not draw too much attention. The cone setup was in the bay so they could pull in and out of it endlessly. Will skidded across the ground, beating his hands against the steering wheel. The crew sat in the back and yelled at him, stressed him out, played sounds of gunfire over the radio. It wasn't until he could do it flawlessly and consistently in the cones that C even let him try it in the actual cover. If he broke it, C wasn't so sure he could fix it.

After two full weekends of pulling in and out of cones, C let him at the cover. Doc posted on the street to watch for traffic and would signal to shut down the door if needed. They took it slow at first, feeling the space, the locking mechanism, the timing of the switch from the stands to the roof rack. The rear door of the truck body swung upwards at the push of a button that Will hit on the visor. He crawled into it, letting the bumper wheels on each side guide the van walls. He slowed on instinct where the front of the van would have hit the tarp and there was a gentle tap of the rubber stoppers hitting the grill plate.

"Good. Now press the lift." C gestured to the buttons on the visor but Will's hand was already there. The clamps on the ceiling of the cover pushed downward, pinching in as they caught the roof mount.

"One, two, three." Will counted the seconds out loud. The hydraulics whirred as the cover shifted into place, "four, five." He inched forward and the sound of scraping metal rang out. The cover stuttered lightly. Will slammed on the breaks.

"You counted too fast." C shook his head. "Five full seconds to clear the ground. Drop it and pull out. Try again."

Will sighed. "Why can't we start a timer when we pull in?"

"The cops aren't going to wait for you to start a timer. You need to know exactly how long you have. Again." Will pressed another button on the visor and the hydraulic reversed. The windshield of the cover slowly dropped out of alignment. He waited for the sounds to stop and started to back out slowly. Out and around the lot again he pulled in at the same speed.

"Good."

Will pressed the lift again. "One, two, three." He counted slower. "Four, five." He pulled forward. The cover cleared the ground and the van moved forward. Will let out a sigh of relief and stopped the truck before the back wall of the bay.

"Better. Again."

For the next six hours, Will cycled in and out of the cover, playing with the lifting mechanism and finally driving around the block with the cover on. Finally, they broke for the day.

"We'll come back to it. Tomorrow." Will gave a light nod and packed his stuff.

* * *

Doc sat at the table finishing a beer and checking news sites. News from the last job had fallen off the headlines to be replaced with celebrity news. He was always nervous they would be identified by some slip-up or facial recognition. His free time had mostly been eaten up with scanning the news, the blogs, the fan pages, looking for anyone that might be close to figuring them out.

"You good in here?" C popped his head in from finishing putting the bay back together.

"Yeah, just keeping an eye on things." Doc kept his attention on his computer.

"Anyone close yet?"

"Nah, last I saw they were trying to match our eyes to a bunch of different celebrities." He had taken the unofficial role of public security and C told him he was grateful to hand over the job. C walked over to the mini-fridge and grabbed a beer. He pulled out a chair and plopped down, cracking open the can.

"How're your ribs?"

"Better. Still a little sore if I press on them, but bearable." He poked at his side.

"Glad to hear it." Doc switched over to a private blog that had taken on quite a following when he posted conjectures on how the PII charger worked.

"How do you feel about this kid?" Though C was in charge, he made a point of checking on group decisions with everyone else. Doc was always appreciative. He could tell that C had known T before this whole thing picked up. They had a chemistry that went beyond professional and now with this new kid that came out of nowhere, he figured there was history there making him the only true stranger. It kind of defeated the whole letter title but Doc didn't want to challenge it. He was content.

"He seems a little green but I think he'll get there." Doc broke away from his computer. "Do you trust him?"

C took a long breath. "Yes. I think he's in the same spot we were all in and as you could tell he's a fan so I think he wants to do well."

"Wanting to do well and doing well are very different things."

"Well, you gotta have one to get to the other. He's got it in him, just needs to get it out." C put back a large swallow of beer.

"It'll work out. If not, we just go to jail, no biggie." Doc smiled. He had come to terms with the risk, it seemed to be the way the world worked now, and he was done following the rules. It had become a means to an end, and the real end was doing good, true good. The mini surgery he did during the robberies was cool, but he always felt a little bad. It was his idea to start getting ketamine and fentanyl and giving it before the incision, to make it easier on them. Plus, it cut down on the screaming. As states slowly started decriminalizing all drugs it was easier and easier to find high-quality pure medication. He followed the dosing that hospitals used for sedation in patients that needed to be intubated, and premixed them in the van before each job after he got a look at the target and could eyeball their weight.

Doc was young. Only twenty-two, the youngest in the group with one of the most important jobs, and he regularly thought he was in over his head. He had medical training, enough to treat the wounded, and a basic knowledge of anatomy, but he was not a doctor. He had no degrees, no college-level understanding of enzymes and neuro-functions. He was low on the medical scale, an Army medic. Well, ex-Army medic. There was some difficulty adapting to the high and tight life and his chain of command was not what he had expected. A bunch of Hoorah, American cock suckin', boogaloos. It was not his scene. A Sergeant First Class went after him one day for not keeping his equipment the way the Army wanted it. Doc disagreed. The SFC disagreed with Doc's disagreement. Doc tried to disagree with the series of disagreements but, after a lot of cursing, his existing record, and a fair amount of bureaucracy, it earned him a Less-Than-Honorable Discharge. It was bittersweet. He was sick of the hierarchy of the Army and by association the government, but all he wanted to do was be on the front lines of something. He had applied to medical school and the

Army was his payment plan. When that fell through like a brick, he had to pivot. Now, a year and a half into school, if he didn't pay, he would be out. The way he saw it, the people they were taking money from might as well be the same people he paid when he signed his tuition check. If they didn't want to pay education taxes, he would see to it personally. As C always says, 'fuck em.'

"It'll work out." C drummed a little on the table. "How are we doing on drugs?"

"We have enough for two jobs. I'll resupply after the next one."

"Cool." The two of them sat in silence for a minute.

"Alright." Doc finished his beer. "I have some real work to do so I'm gonna head home."

"This isn't real work?"

"This is a made-up fantasy world."

"Hmm, you're right. But here we're kings."

15 | PROSTHETICS

(Three years ago)

"Hello, again." A head tilted into the doorway.

"Oh. Hi, Mark." C and El popped their heads up from reading to greet the intruder.

"Sorry to bother you, but my sister brought some homemade cookies for Jimmy and we wanted to see if you wanted any."

"Oh, I just finished lunch. I'm pretty full." C looked to El.

"Oh no, I'm good. Thanks."

Mark entered the room and headed for the counter with a plate of cookies. "Well, I can leave some for when Charlie wakes up."

El put her book down and her hand up. "I'm sorry. He's on a non-PO diet for right now. We don't want to tempt him. But thank you."

Mark's joy diminished a bit. "Oh. Okay. Well, we're just next door, as you know. If you change your mind." He turned on his heel and walked out with a muted smile.

C gave El a look to which she shrugged her shoulders and threw out her hands.

"He's just trying to be nice." C set his book down and stood up.

"I know, but that's the fourth time he's come in today. If we accept, he won't stop."

"I feel bad for him."

El groaned.

"His kid lost an arm."

"Yeah, we're all having a hard time."

C walked out into the hallway and caught Mark before he entered his room.

"Hey, Mark. We'll take a couple cookies, if you're still offering."

Mark spun around and his goofy smile sprung back up. He was a tall, lanky man with well-combed blonde hair and a pair of wire frame glasses that were too small for his face. He wore a button-down shirt that was nicely pressed and tucked in. Generally, he looked like the guy that measures his neighbors' hedge sizes to make sure they are in regulation with the HOA.

"Oh wonderful. They really are quite good. My sister's famous recipe. Been making them for years. You'll love them."

C took the plate and looked at the cookies. They were an odd shade of gray and the paper plate was heavier then it should have been for the number of cookies on it.

"Thanks. They look great." C smiled politely. He redirected. "How's Jimmy doing? You said earlier you guys were having a meeting about the prosthetic?"

"Oh, yes. We just finished it. Before the cookies arrived. I tell you the technology that they have now is just wonderful!"

"That's great. I'm sure Jimmy is very excited for it."

"Oh, yes. He absolutely is. I tell you, for a fourteen year old he is really just taking this like a champ." He swung his fist for emphasis.

"I'm curious what company is making the prosthetic? I work in Bot production and we have some subsidiaries that build those arms."

"Well, to be honest I'd have to look at the packet again. They used to produce this product that was like an armband around your forearm that could record the electrical output of muscles as you moved your hand around. It was kind of like how your Gesture PIN for your PII works but this was long before those things came out. It was meant to interface with computers but never really found the right market and the company shifted the technology to prosthetics." He paused himself and shook his head. "Oh, look at me sounding like an expert. I'm just parroting what the specialist said."

"Hmm. Interesting. It might be a company that we acquired a while back actually. It was called the M-Band. The company was Myos."

"Yes, yes that was it!"

"Oh good. I know some of the guys from that team. You're in good hands."

"Wonderful! I will pass on the good news. Jimmy is getting fitted in a little while."

"Well, tell him I say good luck." C smiled and turned away.

"Oh, absolutely. You tell Charlie I say the same!"

C nodded over his shoulder and continued back to his room. Charlie was still asleep in bed. El had gone back to reading. She looked up when he entered.

"You want a cookie?" C picked one off the plate and bit into it. His teeth only made it a few millimeters in.

16 | Warming Up

"ON THE FUCKING GROUND! FACE THE WALL! BACKS TO ME! HANDS ON YOUR HEAD!" Will stood on a table waving his gun around. The light from his headlamp whipped around the space. "You, in the corner! If I see you looking at me one more time I'm gonna put so many holes in you the coroner won't have anything left to drain." An over-built man in a gray t-shirt turned around cautiously and put his forehead against the wall. He breathed slowly, his eyes shifting rapidly, suddenly realizing that it doesn't matter how many days he went to the gym, he can't punch a bullet.

Will scanned the room and hopped off the table. He walked to the front door and placed a "Closed" sign on the glass. Behind him, C and Doc were man-handling a guy in Psych Locks onto a counter. He looked around the bank and counted. There was one employee behind the counter, and two on the floor. He was missing one. The woman with the red hair. She had come in last that morning to complete the four-employee team for the day. Will looked to the door next to the front desk and reviewed his training. Employees in the back office were a process. He had to get the code from one of the employees in the front and if they declined there wasn't a lot beyond scare tactics he could do. It was ideal of course to have eyes on all employees but if the time to get back there was greater than the time it took for them to call the police, it was better to just take note and hustle. He did another sweep of the lobby and caught a shadow moving in the dark behind a cubicle divider. He wandered over and peeked his head around to find a middle-aged white woman with frizzy red hair held back with a hairband. She looked up with tightly squinted eyes, blinded by the headlamp, and shaking lightly. Will smiled under his mask. Easy.

Along with the four employees there were only three customers in the bank, including the one that was about to be operated on. The target was short and stocky with a custom-fit suit and pointed brown shoes. His hair was combed over and the computer case he was carrying retailed for just over three thousand dollars. C did a lot of research on high-end men's accessories and could tell a faux Coach bag from half a block away or the visual difference between three editions of an Omega Speedmasters and how much they cost to the dollar. Then again, it was crucial to not waste missions on some hack with a Chinese-made tie and a pair of Walmart's best on his feet.

With Angiocoin running the middle class, bank patrons had split into two distinct parties: the bottom of the lower class were there to deal with fines, back taxes, collections—basically all things that the government required federal currency for. The other patrons were the rich, who were forced to be there by the new laws to complete all their financial transactions. Telling them apart was, generally, the easiest part of the job.

The manager of the bank was tied with paracord to a swivel chair and was being whipped around by T who gave him another push every ten seconds or so between typing away at the terminal. The guy looked like he might repaint his suit and the tough-guy attitude that got him put in the chair was rapidly wearing off. C had finished getting the PIN and was handing it to T.

"He's doing good." T watched Will peek through the glass door as he plugged in the gesture tracker. C checked his watch.

"Yeah, not bad." C turned around and admired Will's energy. "I was surprised he came out of his shell that much. In the training, it took a while to get him fired up."

T reached over and gave the manager another spin.

"How's he doing?" C nodded to the manager who was bearing down with his eyes closed.

"Oh, he's being a big tough boss man, isn't he?" T spoke to him in baby talk and then looked at C and rolled his eyes. "Tell Doc this one's gonna blow."

C let out a chuckle and checked his watch again. "Two minutes." The team echoed back.

C walked back to the man where Doc was about to make the first incision and grabbed a hold of the guy's arm. Doc started cutting. From across the room, Will froze in place and locked his eyes on the guy's wrist as blood poured out. The red shined brutally in the focus light. He watched C take a large syringe and suck up thirty or so milliliters of blood which he then pressed into the top of the PII charger. Will's head spun a bit from the gore. Everything felt just like the days of training that he had put in at HQ with the team, but the blood all of a sudden made it so much more real. He watched a stream of it pour off the table into a small puddle on the ground. When they trained, Doc and C mostly talked through this part as it didn't require any of Will's attention, but watching them move now in the zone was incredible, their hands looked like they were from one person, handing this, switching that, holding this. They had practiced this to the millimeter.

Will shook his head from the daze and resumed his rounds. The muscle man in the corner was obeying, his hands interlaced on top of his head. The other customer in the bank was an older woman, maybe seventy-five with white hair and pearl earrings. She looked genuinely terrified and Will was concerned she might have a heart attack. As he made his way around the velvet ropes where the line normally stood, he walked past her, stepping over her legs. He leaned down until he was inches from her ear. He could smell the makeup she had caked on that morning through his mask."You will go home today," he mumbled quietly. She opened her eyes and tried to see him in her peripheral vision without moving her head but he had walked away.

Doc had packed his bags and was running out the door. C gave G the go-ahead and he also made his way out, grabbing the "Closed" sign as he did. He hopped in the driver's seat and started it up; he didn't hear sirens yet but the police scanner on the dash started talking of activity in their area. As he sat in the seat, he noticed how much he was sweating. It was eighty degrees outside and the black beanie was warmer than it looked. He contemplated taking it off but knew C would have a fit. Up the stairs, T ran out the door with a huge grin on his face, pulling a length of paracord from the end. Will could imagine the guy in the chair spinning like a top as the 20 feet of rope uncoiled itself, whipping the chair in the opposite direction. C followed quickly behind, taking a couple of last looks around the bank and pulling out the wood from the door lock. The side door of the van swung open.

"Start pullin'." T handed the rope to Doc and together they wound it up and dropped it in the well next to the door.

"What's that smell?" Doc looked at his glove and noticed there were moist streaks across it. T took a long deep sniff and exhaled, satisfied.

"That's the smell of a hundred bucks."

"He didn't!" Doc said wide-eyed in disbelief. T smiled aggressively as the van pulled away. "Dammit, the way he was when we came in, I thought he had total control over his GI tract."

T laughed and mimicked the manager in a ridiculous, deep tough-guy voice, "You better pack up and turn around, you picked the wrong bank, I have three guns in the back." The two of them laughed.

"Did you pull the scissors on him?"

"Hell yeah, I did." He switched his mimicking voice to small and terrified. "Pl… please sir, I just don't want any trouble, I'll do anything."

Will chimed in. "I *knew* I saw you pull out scissors. What was that for?"

Sirens rang in the distance.

"Here's the thing, G." Will tensed, forgetting that they only knew him as G. "A little nausea always levels the playing field, especially when dealing with wanna-be hard asses. So I bring this here line of paracord, hand one end to the guy, and make him tuck his knees to his chest." T demonstrated. "And then I start spinning real fast. By the time the guy realizes he's getting tied up, it's too late. Old Docy and I had a bet that I could make someone puke by the time we packed up." Doc shook his head in disbelief.

"And the scissors?"

"That's the fun part." T leaned forward. "Everyone is scared of crazy people. You see them on the street and you walk around, horror movies take place in asylums. What you are really scared of is the uncertainty. Society behaves by a set of rules and you are comfortable because you assume everyone else will follow those rules. But if you make someone believe that you are unaware of the rules, they get very uncomfortable. Now, we're only allowed one gun, right?" He asked it as a rhetorical question but C answered from the passenger seat.

"Right."

T squinted his eyes at the back of C's head and continued. "Yes, I could pull out a knife and do that whole thing, but people have seen it before. Plus, if something happens and someone accidentally gets stabbed then we have an issue. Only one stabbing per mission, right Doc?" He slapped Doc's knee across from him who smiled shallowly. "So, if I take out a pair of scissors, hold 'em up like Psycho." He reached in his bag, snatched them out of their pocket, and threw an arm around C's neck from the back. "And say something like 'Listen here buddy.'" He spoke in a high, crackling voice and breathed in C's ear as he held the scissors up to his neck. "'You're gonna sit in that chair right now or we're gonna have an issue.'" He breathed heavier and licked his lips sickeningly. Will laughed as C smiled and rolled his eyes. T cackled and sat back in his seat. "The lip licking is the most important part. Even if they can't see your face, they can hear it. Make someone uncomfortable, they'll do whatever you want just to get away."

* * *

The van pulled off a service road next to the highway and drove under the overpass. A semi-abandoned construction site had left the area desolate. As the van pulled in, Will and C reached out of the window to grab their sideview mirrors. They popped out of place and were set in the center of the cab. It was a nifty little trick that Will's father had installed; that way the cover could be as tight as possible. They squeezed in slowly. The police scanner on the dash was wild with traffic looking for a plain white Ford van heading south on the highway. It would be a minute before reports from traffic cameras saw that it had pulled off the first exit and headed north on the same highway. Enough time for them to pick up the cover and get back on the road, once again heading south. Just a little loop-de-loop for good measure. Eventually, there might be a report of the van getting off the exit near the construction but it would have disappeared after that. Surprisingly, people don't really pay attention to their surroundings no matter how many alerts are put out. As long as cars continued to drive themselves, people would get notifications, take a brief look up at the road, and then get back to their scheduled programming.

Will counted the clicks as the cover sealed to the van and pushed his thumb into the button to start raising it. Motors whirred all around them as they sat silently trying not to distract the new driver from hitting his marks. T was busy typing away at a laptop on a little desk space they had built for him. After a timed five seconds, Will started pulling away knowing the jack stands were at least clear of the ground. It would take another ten for the stands to retract all the way and the top braces to click into place. The most noticeable detail was the double windshield. There was talk at some point to rig the van's windshield to retract or fall forward or something so there would only be the truck's but it never came to fruition. As long as they kept the bottom glass crystal clear and the top glass a little dusty it wasn't an issue, but they weren't stopping for gas anytime soon. Will pulled back up on the highway and headed back to the office.

* * *

Back in the garage, they unloaded gear. Doc dumped his bag out into a bucket to be filled with a bleach solution and Will unloaded scuba masks from a case and checked oxygen tanks. T immediately got to work sitting on the couch. C had explained everything about the aftermath, but Will was still not super confident on every part. He guessed that's why he had his job and they had theirs.

The idea was that most rich people didn't keep very much of their assets as liquid cash. Instead, they were heavily invested in markets: stocks, bonds, money markets, equities, annuities, Angiocoin, etc. T needed access to all of those accounts. The PII charger could keep the device "alive" for a little while, but eventually the blood cells would die and it would start to run out of usable electrolytes to keep power. In order to maintain it for the ride back, which could be up to an hour, Doc placed IV catheters in everyone's arms and secured them with Coban which they wore during the whole mission. These could be readily drained when the charge on the PII was starting to get low (the orange light started pulsing), and the old blood could be dumped and replaced. With the combination of the PII and the saved gesture PIN, T could access pretty much any account the target had. He stayed away from small business accounts so as not to fuck over the little guys at the bottom of the food chain, but the man's life savings? Greenlight.

As T typed away on the couch, Will helped unload the rest of the gear. He pulled the clip out of his pistol, popped the chambered round out, and pushed it back into the magazine. A long time ago, his father took him shooting and when they got home he sat him down and gave him a talk about weapon storage. "Never store a round in the chamber. The time it takes to cock it when you need to is worth the funeral you don't have to go to if it accidentally goes off. Anyone who says there's no time to cock it is either dumb or has a complex." Will smirked to himself. He set the weapon on the rack in the safe.

Doc stood at the sink in the corner scrubbing at his array of tools, picking flakes of dried blood off the handle of his scalpel. The black roll floated on the surface, above the sunken metal tools in a bucket of bleach. C had found an old farm sink at an auction some years back and it sat in his shed for a long time before this whole thing started. When Doc needed a bigger area to thoroughly wash the DNA off his equipment, C and T carried the thing in and got it set up, but not without an extensive debate. The problem being that C was a handyman, and T thought he was a handyman.

"Will, give me a hand out here," C called from the bay. Will spun away from the safe and jogged towards the door. As he passed the couch, Sam stuck his leg out catching Will's back leg and making him stumble. Sam snorted a laugh without looking away from his computer.

"Ass." Will smiled and shook his head.

In the bay, C was spreading out a large tarp behind the truck with the van inside. Will raced to a corner and helped him pull it even. They grabbed the corners and walked the tarp up to the truck, climbed up on the back tires, and pulled it over the roof.

"How was it?," C grunted as he whipped his arm to get more slack.

"Umm, yeah. It was okay. Definitely, the biggest thing I've done."

"That one was pretty standard. You got lucky that your first one was so easy."

"Yeah. The guy barely put up a fight for his PIN."

"You'd be surprised how little people do. When the heat's on, the soft melt."

They tied the tarp under the front bumper. There was not really a reason to cover the truck as no one was looking for it, but C had a fear that the landlord, or someone important, might stroll in one day for an inspection and look too close at the rig.

"We've had, I think, two that have given us a real hard time but once you wave a gun in someone's face they change their mind. The second guy kept resisting and the old G shot a round next to his ear. Even with the silencer he probably has permanent hearing loss, but he gave up the PIN."

"I thought I wasn't supposed to shoot unless we were in danger?"

"You're not. I told you, the last guy was… unstable."

They tied the back of the tarp to the back bumper.

"So do you have any questions? Anything go different from the training?"

"I don't think so. I mean, I guess… Do you ever feel bad about taking these people's entire livelihood? T said he pulls all their savings from their stocks too. That's pretty brutal."

"Ehh, fuck 'em. Someone somewhere will bail them out. Rich people have rich friends. If they have to sell their ten million dollar house and their private jet then I call it a win."

"But how do you know they have the structure to fall back on?"

"I don't. I see they have nice things, they like to flaunt their wealth, I assume they have enough money to make our operation worth it. I was wrong once. Our third gig, the guy apparently had spent a ton of newfound money on a Rolex and the Armani suit he wore and everything else was encrypted in the Russian's version of Angiocoin that T was too nervous to get into. The guy was also a massive dick. He was the first one that gave us trouble getting his PIN. He spit on me before we could get the rag in his mouth. Like I said, fuck'em."

Will walked back into the office. Doc was laying his tools in the safe. Sam had closed up his computer and placed it on the shelf before heading to the bathroom.

"Hey, T."

"What's up, man?" he called from behind the half closed bathroom door.

"Oh, I was curious about the power thing. How do you cut the whole building off so quick?"

"Ahh." The toilet flushed and the sink ran. T kicked the door further open while checking his teeth in the mirror.

"Essentially," he walked out of the bathroom, "there is a switch on the city side of the control box outside the building. The technicians use it to turn everything off and on for some input/output tests or when they are doing a big rewiring and don't want to blow themselves up. Flip it and nothing goes in or out."

"It's that simple?"

"Well, they lock it."

"Oh. Then how do you…"

T laughed. "You think a little padlock is gonna stop Ol' Bessy over there?" He pointed to a large pair of bolt cutters with Hello Kitty duct tape wrapped around the handles.

"But still, that seems like it's too easy."

"I'll tell you kid, some of the guys doin' the city's electrical work," he leaned in slightly, "not the cream of the crop. If they didn't color code everything, the city would be on fire daily."

Will chuckled lightly and rolled his eyes.

"Hey, jokes aside, kid. Good job." T put his hand out. Will gave it a shake.

"Thank you." He smiled. Satisfied.

17 | THE UNKNOWN

(Three Years Ago)

"Hey, Dad, what happens when you die?"

Charlie was sitting up—the hospital bed at a seventy-degree angle, and a stack of pillows doing the rest to hold him in place. The faint sound of air hissing buzzed around the room, emitting from the high-flow nasal cannula on his face, trying to force oxygen into his body. The bedding had recently been changed and an EKG electrode clung to the corner of the draw sheet, having made its way through the washing, bleaching, and inspection of the laundry company, packaged and transported to be stretched out and presented as a clean and sterile place to lay the healing and the recovering, the diseased and wounded.

The square white sticker with a metallic button was a relic of the last patient who inhabited these sheets. Clearly, someone whose heart warranted a picture: perhaps a nice old man whose young granddaughter clung to his hand as he received a routine check of his pacemaker. To her, the wires and tubes would seem foreign and terrifying, and seeing her grandfather tied to a machine would surely make her think he was on his way out. Perhaps the electrode was from a drug addict. A cokehead who sat and listened to a legitimately concerned nurse explain for the third time that his heart was like any other muscle and that the more he raced it, the thicker it got, shrinking the chambers and reducing the amount of blood it can pump. He would take note and see her again in three weeks for the same problem. Maybe the sticker was from some other kid, one with a congenital heart defect and he too, lay in a bed, clinging his fists to the sheet as one nurse stuck him in the arm with an IV and the other placed electrodes all over his chest. Was the patient alive still? The last person that sticker was attached to? Was the last signal that electrode picked up not a signal at all but the absence of one? A whole world, life, existence, left behind by a small white sticker with a metal button.

Charlie looked curiously out of the corner of his eye at his father who sat in a chair to the right of the bed up against the air conditioner, absent and focused, staring at the sticker on the side of the sheet. He said nothing and did not move. Charlie tightened his fingers, squeezing the sheet in his fist. A light blanket sat covering his legs up to his stomach and a hospital gown wrapped itself around his shoulders. Wires climbed up his sleeves and down his collar, connected to electrodes that stuck to his skin. Under the gown his chest rose and fell with tremendous effort, the intercostal muscles pulling the ribs to their limit, the abdomen taking the rest of the burden. A light sheen of sweat painted itself over his body, his skin light and delicate. Outside the room was quiet, at this time of night the halls were stalked by only a handful of nurses, doctors, techs, and CNAs, who fueled themselves with coffee and energy drinks as they switched between updating charts and shopping online for new shoes. A short

Venezuelan lady pushed a cart past the door, armed with a broom and mop and other cleaning essentials, dragging behind her a tall white tower on wheels with a long ultra-violet bulb for convenient microscopic genocide.

C continued to stare at the bed. His eyes were wide and focused but everything around them was falling apart. His elbow propped on the armrest, his thumb, pressed under his cheekbone, his first two fingers holding up his head at the temple. Dark lines were cradled under his eyelids and the corners of his mouth fell from exhaustion. Still, he said nothing and did not move. The clothes he wore were old, unwashed. His green long sleeve shirt had three buttons at the top though none were fastened, and his jeans wrinkled with a slight tear at the knee. His shoes were tumbled over next to the chair and the cotton of his socks was becoming see-through at the toes. Charlie sighed and redirected his attention forward, once again trying to fall back asleep but failing miserably. Except for the hissing of air, and a faint and consistent beeping from down the hall, it was silent. Time passed.

"I don't know." C rubbed his eyes coming out of his daze. "No one knows." His breathing was steady. He frequently noticed how much we take the ease of breathing for granted while he watched his son.

Charlie looked at him, surprised that he had even heard him. "Someone in my class said you go to Heaven but everyone told him that was stupid." C chuckled.

"Yeah, well. Some people think that." He took a deep breath. "There are stories. Stories of incredible, wondrous worlds that exist, filled with everything you could ever want and all your friends and family, and there was a man with a beard to sit and judge you based on how good you were in life and he sends you to that incredible world," he shrugged and shook his head, "or, if you were bad, to a place of evil and torture. But that's only a fairytale." C swallowed. "A fairytale that parents told to their kids so often they started to believe it themselves." He was talking to the electrode. "Some people just clung to it so hard because they weren't smart enough, or brave enough for the alternative."

"What's that?"

A long pause. C looked at the ground and shrugged. "The Unknown." He clenched his jaw and gestured non-descriptly. "That's the alternative. Leaping off a rock of all you know, all that you can imagine, into the absolute darkness of the void." His matter-of-fact voice trailed off as he spoke.

"So there's nothing?" Charlie started to panic. "When I die I'm just going to sit in the dark forever?" His breathing increased which incited a coughing fit. C quickly sat up and slid over Charlie's side, grabbing his hand. He had been awake for over forty-eight hours and was not in the mindset to be explaining the concept of death to a seven-year-old who probably doesn't feel too far from it. His tangent was the result of sleep deprivation and many hours of hopelessness. This most recent stay in the hospital had been the longest at just over four weeks. They could treat the symptoms for a few months but they always came back. The difficulty breathing, the coughing fits. It was getting worse.

"No, no, no, no, no. buddy, shhh, shhhhhh." He waited for the coughing to subside, getting an emesis bag from behind the mattress just in case, and stroked Charlie's hair. After a few seconds or so, the coughing fit stopped and Charlie regained his composure.

"Listen, buddy, the truth is we just don't know. We can make guesses and hope and dream and fear but no one knows. The best I can tell you is it's probably a lot like before you were born. Do you remember that?"

Charlie shook his head.

C thought for a minute. "It's truly the last great mystery of all time. Somewhere that, one day, a long time from now when you are old and gray, you will get to set off on a journey to and solve the mystery, explore the real final frontier." He spoke heroically, like a barkeep sending an adventurer out on a quest. "You can finally see what all the fuss is about. It's never something to fear, it's something to prepare for, in here." C tapped him on the forehead. He took a beat, looking into his son's eyes, trying to telepathically send whatever strength he had left. He folded his lips into a small smile. "I'll tell you a secret. Can you handle it?"

Charlie smiled and nodded subtly.

"This is real deal adult stuff, are you sure?"

Charlie nodded more intently.

C leaned in close. "Okay." He looked around deliberately to make sure no one was listening.

Charlie giggled.

"When you watch a scary movie and then go to sleep what kind of dream do you have?"

"A nightmare?"

"Right, and if I spend all day talking about purple elephants, what do you think is going to be in your dream that night?"

Charlie giggled again. "Purple elephants."

"Yes. So if I told you your whole life that when you die there is going to be a dark tunnel with a light at the end and if you follow the light you'll be in a warm place surrounded by your friends and family, what do you think you will see when you die?"

"A dark tunnel?"

"Exactly. So for the next hundred years before you die," C gave him a smirk, "I want you to think about all of the best things in your life. All your friends at school, all of your toys, our house, playing in the backyard, waffles with syrup, trips to the movies, swimming at the beach, standing on top of mountains, your family, your mom, and me. Think about them every day as much as you possibly can and try to remember as many good things as you can, that way when you finally die, that will be all you see, forever."

Charlie smiled big and looked at his hands. C stared at him hard, trying to mentally photograph every inch of his face, trying to remember as much as he could.

"Okay, dad, I'll do that."

"Good, now how about some ice cream?"

"But it's late. The nurse said I'm supposed to go to sleep."

"Fine," C said standing up, "I'll just have to get some for myself and you can sleep while I eat it." He started to walk out of the room.

"No, no, I want ice cream!"

C stopped and looked back. He smiled. "Alright, fine. Quit hounding me about it."

Charlie laughed.

The night ended with ice cream wrappers littering the table and Charlie fast asleep sitting in bed. C slumped in a chair with his head resting on the edge of the bed, a hand on Charlie's.

* * *

"Charlie" was still written on the whiteboard in big awkward letters, now the only thing tying him to this room, to this world. C's eyes were fixated on the name, wide and unmoving. He had been picking at his fingernail but had since frozen in position. The room was in disarray, plastic wrappers from various medical supplies were scattered around the floor. The monitor flashed visual alarms stating that there was no patient connected. Outside the room, the hospital carried on its daily tasks. Nurses gave medications, doctors held consults, CNAs changed out Foley catheters. A short Venezuelan lady packed up her belongings and clocked out. The center of the room was empty. A large area where the bed had been was now filled with the ends of cords and tubes that were draped on the ground, still connected at one end to their respectful hubs and monitors. C continued to stare, motionless. Within the threshold of the door, the world had stopped. Time stood still. A nurse broke the frozen timeline.

"Sir, I'm sorry but if you are able to, we have a day room down the hall that you are welcome to sit in, but we really need this room for another patient." There was no answer. "Sir?" C was a photograph. The nurse inhaled and exhaled sharply and walked out.

A beat. Like pressing play on a pause screen, C took in air sharply. Apparently, he had been holding his breath though he didn't realize. A few more agonal gasps followed. He scanned the room in terror as if he had been transported there from another time. He hyperventilated, unable to catch his breath. He looked at the wall behind where the bed was and dove to the floor. He grabbed the oxygen mask that lay on the floor and cranked up the knob on the wall meter. Fifteen liters of oxygen a minute flowed through the mask as he took increasingly longer, deeper breaths. He put his back to the wall and slid down, sitting amongst the trash on the floor.

"Hey, honey?" A familiar voice came from the door.

C looked up to see his wife standing in the doorway, her eyes were bloodshot and the skin around it was red and irritated. A small streak of makeup ran off her left eyebrow, a spot she missed when she cleaned herself up in the bathroom.

"What are you doing?"

"Couldn't breathe." C said quickly in between breaths.

Elizabeth walked into the room and sat down next to him. She looked at her husband sitting on the floor of the hospital room sucking in oxygen through a pediatric non-rebreather, the one that had been strapped to their son right before he was intubated. She offered up a hand. C took the mask off and handed it to her. She put it to her face and took a few deep breaths.

"We have to go home," she sighed and laid her forearm over her knee, her wrist hanging loose with the mask resting in it. "We have a lot to take care of and the nurses are starting to get antsy. Apparently, this is the last open room."

C took another deep breath, in through the nose, out through the mouth, and looked around the room. "Okay."

Elizabeth stood and offered a hand to C. He looked at it, studied its grooves and ridges, noted the thin lines of mascara that streaked the side of the middle finger. He took it and let her pull him up. She was strong.

18 | To The Crew

A man in a gray suit stepped out of a gray sedan in the Modern Moving parking lot and made eye contact with Will as he dragged on a cigarette next to the garage door. Will gave a small nod and tried to emit a thorny aura, hoping the man would stay far away.

"Hey!" The man threw a hand up as he pulled a bag from the vehicle and made steps towards the garage.

Fuck. Will dropped his cigarette and stepped on it while reaching for the door but quickly realized that looking like you are running away from people promotes suspicion. Will threw a hand up in submission. The man drew closer, even giving a light hop in his step. Will checked the window in his peripheral to ensure the blinds were closed. They always were.

The man's suit was a bit too small for his frame, possibly purchased a few too many pounds ago. His red and black striped tie was loose enough to see that the top button was unfastened. His shoes were brown and beaten and a slice of neon green socks peeked out above them. He looked like middle management for which there was no upper.

"Hey, how ya doing?" He was trying to hide his lack of breath.

"Good, sir." Will hoped his limited response would give his intent. It didn't.

"Yeah, I don't really see you guys around too much. Just that van and the box truck that come in and out. You a mechanic shop?"

"Umm, yeah sort of. We do on-location stuff." Will recited the story C had made him memorize for this specific encounter.

"Oh yeah, that's cool. Yeah, a couple of us were curious. No sign or nothin'." He gestured above the door.

Will looked up at the bare space where two bolts once held a sign years ago. He let out a grunt and gave a subtle agreeing nod.

"Yeah, we had a little bet. Buddy of mine said you were launderin' money in there." He let out a chuckle that implied more humor than it should have.

Will offered a light smile.

"Yeah, well." There was a pause that was filled with uncomfortable eye contact. The man gestured with his thumb. "I'm sure you've seen our trucks around. Third biggest transport company in the country. This is the regional corporate office, though." He said it as if he had anything to do with the accolade. "I just run the local payroll system. But we do some industrial moving too. Hell, if you ever need your shop moved... well I guess your whole thing is portable. That's the point. Right?" He gave a physical nudge and wink.

Will scratched his eye and looked at the neighboring building. He assumed a company that big would have a glass office in a tech park somewhere, not a drab block of an industrial park. "Hey, you guys had that executive die a little while back, right? In the heist?" Will tested the waters.

"Oh yeah. James. Guy was a prick. I mean I didn't

143

know him personally, of course. He was up at the top of the ol' food chain there. Spent a lot of time bouncing around the regional offices barkin' orders though." The man leaned in a little. "If you ask me, this 'Cut Wrist Crew' is doin' us all a favor. Keep those rich bastards scared." Will laughed lightly. "Hell, I'd shake their hands. The bar down the road we go to after work has a tribute wall and a drink named after them. I tell ya the day James got merked, there was a few extra shots taken that night." He gave a deliberate wink. "Shame they didn't even take his money. Just collateral damage. I wouldn't mind seeing this place burn a little. I just work here, you know. Some of those higher-ups could use the rustle."

"Yeah, well, to the Crew!" Will stuck his hand out.

"To the Crew!" The man met his hand and gave a firm shake. "Hey, come by the bar some time. It's called Lou's. It's right at the end of the road here. Bit of a biker bar. Good people though."

"I'll check it out." Will smiled hard and gave him a wave as he left.

* * *

"Who was that?" T sent the cue ball hurtling towards the point of the rack at the other end of the table. The balls exploded against each other, clacking and bouncing across the green felt. As they settled, the yellow nine-ball found its way to a side pocket and T shook a fist in victory.

"I don't know. Some guy from the trucking company next door." Will grabbed a cue stick and watched T line up another shot.

"What did he want?" T sent the stick forward,

punching a ball against the bumper and slicing wide away from the pocket. He sighed and knocked the cue against the wood.

"Just curious what we do. I told him the mobile mechanic thing. He took it." Will circled the table eyeing up all the options T had left him. "He's a big fan of ours." Will settled on a long shot along the rail. "Said there was a bar down the road that has a tribute wall?" The cue ball smacked the three and sent it speeding into the back of the pocket. T frowned.

"Yeah, Lou's. We went there once early on. It's alright. Sad place to be too often. C gets a little nervous that someone might recognize his eyes. Doc refuses to go near the place." T grabbed the pole with both hands and gave it a practice swing like a baseball bat. "Lou's is for Losers."

"I know there are a lot of fan groups but it feels different when you're on the receiving end." Will sunk another ball and re-chalked.

"I tell ya when we started this thing it was just for the money." T grabbed his beer off the workbench and took a swig. "Didn't mean for it to become a whole political campaign but the people voted I guess. It's probably kept the cops off us more than we know."

Will missed a bank shot. " What do you mean?"

T chalked his cue stick up and lined up an easy knock-in. "I mean you've seen us on the news. We've become this, like, Robin Hood figure. We have more merch than a ska band. The graffiti, and articles, and conspiracies that support us—it's almost biblical. I think if they brought us down there would be riots." The cue ball followed into the pocket. T dropped his head and silently cursed.

Will started circling again. He grabbed his beer from

the edge of the table and paced as he sipped. "Yeah, I just can't imagine the police visibly allowing it to happen." He measured the angle of a tricky shot between two other balls.

"Ehh, they're just people, too. They have opinions and political views. You know how the country is now. If you don't have servants then you are one. Maybe thirty years ago when there was still a middle class it would be different but we've devolved into the fifteenth century with the kings in the towers and the rest of us in the shit." Will squeezed the cue ball down a narrow slot of balls and put his ball across the table to a far corner pocket. T tilted his head a bit. "I mean after the last job there was an impromptu parade downtown screaming 'eat the rich' with our name on posters." Will jumped the cue ball over the eight but narrowly missed his shot.

T finished his bottle and tossed it in the garbage can near the door. When C had approached him about the project he was hesitant to so overtly steal money. It was an uncharted step in crime that was mostly deemed impossible, which inadvertently ended up being the hook that T was looking for. He and C spent months researching and dialing in all of the security specifications of the PII. Detailed user manuals, patents, pages and pages of FAQs, company statements, brochures, everything. He even interviewed one of the developers that worked on the design floor with a promise to publish him in his obscure tech review blog. They had become absolute experts in the world of the PII. T then reverse-engineered the specs and created the charger. Tinkering was his passion.

When it was just a proof of possibility he was happy, and then the money came in and he was ecstatic. The unseen variable was the public response. At first, T just thought there was some grunge culture that thought it was cool that they were sticking it to the man, but it grew so quickly that no one could stop it. The news networks tried to put a cap on the situation but the public saw through to the pockets of the people writing the copy and dismissed them even more. T was grateful that he was a part of the revolution until he became the revolution. He assumed the only way to end it would be a fiery explosion mid-job or their capture that would lead to a tearing down of the capitol building. He supported either option. He missed a short shot that he cut too hard.

Will cleared two more balls in quick succession but scratched on the third. His voice softened. "Hey T?"

"Yeah man?" T grabbed the cue ball and rolled it around in his hand.

"Do you get nervous?" Will sat against the side of the table.

T set the ball against a ball that teetered on the edge of a pocket and tapped it in. "About losing in pool? Never. They call me the comeback king." No one called him that.

"No, about the job. Like if something goes wrong and the cops do get us."

T stood up and shrugged. "I'll tell ya, man, we've been doin' this for a minute and C is so anal. Something pretty crazy would have to happen. We have contingencies out the ass. You remember training."

Will looked at the floor. "Yeah, but you know, things happen. Someone could get a shot off. Are you ever nervous you could get killed?"

T chuckled. "Me?" He lined up his stick to give the ball a little backspin. "I'm gonna live forever, kid. You can put it on the stone." The cue ball flew off the table.

19 | Shots

"Guarded American" was lifted slightly in blue italic letters above the counter. The fourth-largest bank chain in corporate America had a strong modernism to it that bordered on tacky. Everything looked very... fast. The bank's walls were made up of giant screens which, when the electricity was on, flashed and scrolled with actors who were undoubtedly denied the royalty deals that they should have demanded as they smiled and laughed, walking through the front door of their brand new home with "The lowest interest in the country, guaranteed" loans. Other screens showed the image of a man scanning his wrist at a convenience store checkout which then tiled a couple of hundred times across the screen with claims to have the most POS terminals in the country within three years. It was a bold claim, and probably not going to happen, but the ad looked cool nonetheless.

Now the screens were off, just large black rectangles. The room was very airy and open with only a few counters along the edges and a small water feature in the middle that, when on, if you glanced at it quickly enough, looked like an optical illusion of falling water and horizontal lines. It was donated by the family of a guy who did something important that no one could remember. Or maybe he just had a lot of money. It's often hard to tell the difference.

Initially, the water feature was designed as an infinity pool, flush with the ground, the water flowing seamlessly into the floor. It looked very classy until an otherwise pre-occupied woman walked hastily and efficiently into the fountain, fell the foot and a half to the bottom, and broke her ankle. Now, as the result of a rather lengthy legal case, the feature was surrounded by a low concrete wall with a very out-of-place yellow caution sign bolted to the front of it.

Along the floor were painted black lines that directed traffic to various windows and machines. It created a nice geometric design that mixed art and function so customers felt less like they were being herded. These lines were now empty as maybe a dozen patrons crowded in rows up against the walls with their backs to the center of the room and their hands on their heads. Just in front of the water feature lay a man on the ground who was currently grunting in anger through the towel in his mouth, wriggling away in his metallic hug bands, and generally having a bad time.

"Give me your PIN." The large man above him looked in his eyes, easy and calm.

The man on the ground twisted his wrist around and wiggled his thumb. The light on his PII remained orange.

"Did you just try a fake PIN? You know it flashes green when it registers?"

The man's rage grew, partially mad at himself for trying a stupid trick on these guys who he knew were experts. He attempted a string of curse words, but the towel in his mouth left him grunting unintelligibly. He tried to open his eyes wide but instinctively squinted in the bright headlight that poured over his face. His face was beet red. He knew what was happening. As soon as he saw them walk in he knew who they were, why they were there. He only prayed that they were after someone else.

* * *

"G," C called across the room to Will who was canvasing the front windows, and the people who had huddled down to the left of them. "I need some encouragement over here."

Will hustled to the center and the man heard the indistinguishable sound of a gun being cocked. Will leaned over the man. He smiled under his mask, his eyes squinted above it. The man turned his attention to the new light that shined down on him, a new look of fear creeping across his face. Will tipped his headlamp back slightly so the man could see his eyes. His face went serious, his eyes straightening out, eyebrows ever so slightly furrowed, the bottom lid of his eye tensed. He shoved his gun in between the eyes of the man who went cross-eyed trying to see what he presumed would be his murder weapon.

"I'm not a patient man. And if you don't do what my friend over here tells you, we're going to have an issue."

C made eye contact with Doc and Will and tapped his watch. They nodded.

The man tried to force a serious-looking frown but the obstruction in his mouth made him look ridiculous.

"Or we could kill you and move on to the next guy. We have time."

The man shuddered.

"Alright, if that's how you want it." Will moved his finger from the side of the slide to the trigger. "You sure?"

The man tightened his face, determined to convince himself that Will was bluffing. Will shrugged and pulled the trigger.

The gun clicked. The man's eyes went wide.

Will frowned. "Huh, must have jammed. Give me a second." He turned around and put the loaded clip back in, which he had removed on the way over. He faced the man again and cocked the gun slowly so that the man could see the new bullet slide into place. "There we go, good as new. Now, back to it." He pressed the gun back into the man's forehead which instantly lost all its color. The man shook his head, wide-eyed. He moaned through the towel and shook his hand. "Oh, do we want to try again?" The man nodded. His fingers and hand gestured out his PIN and his PII flashed green. Will smiled. "Thank you."

* * *

C unclasped the armband and ran it over to T who had been trying to shoot the shit with the obviously terrified customer service representative. "They say blue is calming and serene but to me, it just feels like a void of sadness. Don't you agree?" The man huddled in the corner, his whole body shaking. He nodded slowly, unsurely.

"That took longer than I wanted, we gotta double-time here." C set it on the desk and plugged it in.

"Waiting on you, big chief." T took a deep breath and got to work, trying to move as quickly as he could. They had built time into the schedule for difficult targets but when they complied, C usually had a second or two to check in with T. This was not one of those times. C hurried back to Doc who had already given the sedative and made the first incision with Will's help. C reached to take over when the front door was kicked in.

A man in a black long sleeve shirt walked inside. He wore a black beanie and a blue surgical mask across his face. Above his left eye, his brow was scarred and deformed. Slung over his right shoulder was a duffle bag, unzipped with his hand resting inside of it. All four headlamps lit him up like a searchlight.

"Fuck."

The duffle bag dropped to the ground revealing a gloved hand holding an AR-15 firing rounds into the floor around the man lying on the ground as the other hand came up to meet the barrel. Doc, C, and Will dove over the low wall behind them and into the fountain, splashing water across the tile floor. Between the depth of the water and the height of the cement wall, they could tuck down comfortably. T dropped behind the counter and looked to the employee he was trying to make a lasting relationship with who had promptly vagaled down and passed out.

Gunshots riddled the edge of the concrete and up the walls. People screamed and cried. They huddled tighter to each other, grabbing the hands and backs of the total strangers that curled up next to them. The old G sprayed the room, the floor, the screens. Will looked at C with wide eyes. C nodded to him.

"Greenlight."

Will popped up and opened fire. He grazed G once in the right leg just below his hip and dropped back down. G let out a hard grunt and dropped his gun. It bounced on the floor with a mix of plastic and metallic clicks. Will sprung up again over the wall with his pistol white-knuckled out in front of him. The doorway was empty. He caught the tail end of a shadow limping as it disappeared to the right of the front window. Sirens rang in the distance.

"FUCK!" C stood up and looked around. "Fuck, fuck." He looked at his watch. "Fuck it. T! Pack it up." He hopped over the wall and grabbed the edge of the Psych Lock. "Hey, give me a hand here," he waved to Will. "Doc, pack up your shit." Will holstered his weapon behind his back and jumped the wall. He grabbed the other edge of the metal sheet and started to pull. A pool of blood drained out under the man and dark wet patches were forming on his chest and leg. C took a deep breath and closed his eyes. He pulled hard at the Lock which unfolded as Will pulled the other side. The man's lifeless body twisted and fell back to the floor as they pulled the first and second sheet out from underneath him. At least he was doped up. C handed the Psych Locks to Doc who had just finished rolling his tools up.

"Go, now."

Doc nodded and ran for the door. C started towards the desk. "T!"

"Ten Seconds." T quit out of the applications he was running and cleared out the computer. He unplugged the wires and slammed everything into his bag which he lobbed across the counter to C. He pulled himself over and started running for the door. C gestured to Will to leave though he was already at the door. One last look around the room. Bullet holes formed lines above the heads of the customers who were still huddled in their corners. He tilted his head in confusion. Somehow, none of the people around the room seemed to be hit. There was no obvious blood or screams of pain. The bullet holes seemed to be focused on the floor in front of them and the walls above them. The only person who wasn't so lucky was the man they were operating on. C thought for a second, turned, and sprinted to the van.

The sirens were getting closer and Will pulled away the second C's feet we're in, passenger door still open. They sped down the road making a right at a red light to avoid waiting. The police scanner was going crazy with units giving status updates. At one point "white van" made it across the air. C slammed the dashboard.

"Fuckin, Fuck! God damnit!"

"Who was that?" Will had a shakiness to his voice.

"Focus on driving. We need to make it to the cover. Back roads only. Keep to the speed limit. Three-second stops."

Will put his head down and stared at the road ahead. He turned back and forth down side streets, eyes shifting back and forth, ears raised trying to gauge the direction of danger. They pulled out from a neighborhood to a light and looked west across a six-lane road with a guardrail median that ran the length of it. They were a half-mile from the alley with the cover in it. After they crossed the boulevard, they could duck back into the private neighborhood that backed up against the highway and dip down into an industrial lot on the other side where the box truck was. A police car pulled up to the red light at the intersection in front of them heading southbound and stopped. "POLICE" was written in large white letters against a black stripe that ran the length of the vehicle. On the back corner was unit number 509 and in red italics below, there was a reminder to call 9-1-1 if you have an emergency. The cop drummed at his steering wheel and pursed his lips.

Everything froze. Will didn't blink. C didn't blink. The officer was looking at the oncoming traffic ahead, trying to pin down a white van that may be coming in his direction down the main stretch of road. He picked up his radio and broadcasted his post which gargled in on their scanner. Will could feel his heart in his throat. The crew sat silently staring out the windshield at the driver's side of the police car that sat just three lanes away. C looked right, down the open road to the next intersection. To the left, a line of cars waited patiently for the light to change, the drivers staring at their phones while their automated cars received a digital countdown from the traffic light until it turned green.

"Go right." C looked straight forward at the cop. He spoke calmly.

"That neighborhood doesn't have an entrance up there. The only way is straight ahead."

The light turned green and the line of cars started moving across the intersection.

"Go right now!" C lifted off his seat slightly as he yelled. Will slammed on the gas and the wheels sputtered as the vehicle lurched forward out in front of the line of cars approaching from the left. A few honked as Will cranked the wheel to the right and the van almost rolled, tilting out onto two tires. The police officer whipped his head around to see a white van fly out into traffic and bolt down the road behind him. His lights flickered on and the siren yelped. The police scanner in the van lit up with an alert of their location. As the officer tried to swing the U-turn, dozens of drivers had to drop their devices and take control of their steering wheels to make room for the patrol car. The slow reaction paired with the dense column of oncoming cars created a tight jam that the officer had to navigate slowly. The van approached the next intersection.

"U-turn, now." C was bracing himself with his right hand on the handle next to the window and his left hand on the bottom of his seat. Will pulled the wheel to the left and the van stuttered as he slammed on the brakes so as to not take the U going forty miles per hour. A large, oncoming truck had to swerve to the right and slam its brakes to avoid the crash. By the time the cop had made it up to speed heading north, the van passed it on the other side. The officer tried to swing the U-turn hard to make up time but ended up skidding out and landing in a drainage ditch on the far side of the road.

Will made the right turn and disappeared into the twisting neighborhood. The police officer put out the information of which direction they had gone and it wouldn't be long before the courts, circles, and culs-de-sac were crawling with cops. Will decided to bypass some of the finer roads that they would have used to stay hidden in favor of making it through as quickly as possible. A solid wall began running along both sides of the road and turned outwards as the road dropped and the roar of the highway buzzed before them. They ducked under the overpass and traveled two blocks before turning between two warehouses not too different from their own headquarters. There sat their car cover, undisturbed and inviting.

C had hit the button a half block away and the door was open when they got there. Will pulled in faster than he meant to, but he was straight and the rubber stoppers on the inside of the fake grill plate caught them. The shell stuttered forward slightly when Will hit the breaks a little too late. The back door closed, the cover shifted into place, and the truck was off. They flipped around and drove five blocks north to the closest on-ramp where they pulled onto the highway going south, passing the small neighborhood they came out of. The police scanner rambled with officers clearing different sections of the area, all looking for a white van.

* * *

"Is everyone okay?" In all the commotion no one had spoken much and Doc was legitimately nervous that one of them had been shot but was so amped up, they didn't notice. "No one got hit, right?" He looked around at the crew who each gave him a half-assed thumbs up.

"Who the fuck was that!?" Will shifted his eyes between the road and C. The truck bounced along down the highway.

"G." C took a deep breath and rubbed his face. "FUCK!" He punched the dashboard hard enough that Doc thought he heard his hand crack.

"The old G?"

"I don't know how he got the drop on us."

Doc chimed in from the back. "Has he come by the shop at all?"

"I haven't seen him," said T who, out of all of them, spent the most time at their headquarters.

"God fucking damnit!" C was in a rage that seemed dangerous. The police scanner still buzzed away with units clearing sectors of the neighborhoods and they had seen a series of patrol cars speeding up and down the highway though none seemed to pay any attention to them. Will white-knuckled the steering wheel every time an officer popped into his view. At one point the red and blues started flashing behind them and a wave of nausea flooded them all but subsided when the patrol car drove past and pulled someone over that was a half mile up the road.

"How did he know we were going to be there?" Will looked genuinely concerned. This crazed man was out and about with a hell of a vendetta.

"I don't know. I don't fucking know. Once we get back to the garage we can regroup. I need to think for now."

The hum from the road took over.

20 | How

C paced the bay. He racked his brain for any connection that G might have exploited. Doc carried equipment from the van back into the lounge. C watched him walk, awkward, but strong. *Could he?* C scratched at his head and rubbed the back of his neck. He turned and gazed at the wall of tools behind him. Searching.

"Whatcha thinkin'?" T came up behind him and sat on the corner of the drawing table.

C sighed. "I don't know. The only people that knew where we were going were us, Doc, and the kid." C remained staring at the wall, into space. He picked at something on the corner of his nose with his thumb and walked around to the front of the drawing table, behind T, resting his palms on it. He leaned closer, tilting his head to keep an eye on the door to the lounge. "It couldn't be Doc, right?"

"I can't imagine. Doc hated that guy." They both looked straight ahead at the wall of tools.

"That's what I thought."

"Yeah, no, Doc is super careful. He already feels like he's in over his head. Every time G stepped out of line he would tell me how uncomfortable he was."

C took a breath.

T continued, "What about this new kid?" He nodded to the lounge.

159

"I don't know. It can't be."

"Of course it can, this paranoid drug addict gets booted, finds this kid that you used to know, puts some idea in his head about how you are a horrible guy. That you kicked him out for no reason, and plans to get you caught."

"But the kid put himself in the line of fire? No way."

"Did you notice the bullet holes? They were all above us in the walls, he didn't hit anyone. He must have staged this little shootout, faked getting hit, and dipped."

"But the kid was with us the whole time. If he planned it he would get caught too. What's the payoff?" C took a sharp inhale and made another point. "And also, G doesn't know me, where I come from. How did he manage to find this random kid from my past?"

"I don't know." T shook his head, "It just seems like too much of a coincidence."

They stood in silence.

"Hey C!" Will called out from the lounge.

The two men turned their heads towards him in sync. Their eyes were straight and their mouths blank, their faces heavy.

"Uhh, we are out of cleaner for the van, did you want me to go pick some up?"

"Yeah, you know the kind?"

"Doc wrote it down for me."

"Go ahead."

Will turned back to the lounge awkwardly. C and T looked back at each other. C sighed.

"So what are we going to do?"

"About the kid? Nothing right now. But I have an idea for G."

* * *

The phone rang.

Officer: Precinct 108

C: Hello, officer. I'd like to report some information about the bank shooting this morning. (His voice echoed in the phone.)

Officer: Can I have your name, sir?

C: I'd rather report anonymously if that is possible.

Officer: Okay. (keyboard clicking) What information do you have?

C: Well, I was getting lunch in the area and I saw who I think was the shooter running out of the building.

Officer: Where were you, sir?

C: I was at Ken's Deli on the corner. So, I saw him run out and pull his mask down to catch his breath.

Office: Do you remember anything defining?

C: Well, I think I might know the guy.

Officer: You know the shooter personally?

C: Well I met him a couple times as a friend of a friend. I don't remember his name but I can tell you what he looks like.

Officer: Sir, if you have a description of his face we would really like you to come down to the station and give a description for a sketch artist.

C: I'd really rather not be associated, but you can give the artist this recording. He is maybe five foot nine with round green eyes, short military brown hair, sort of olive skin, a larger hooked nose that might have been broken a couple times. He has a sharp jawline with a pointed chin. He usually has a light beard but it's patchy. He has a scar above his left eye that took away a good chunk of his eyebrow and a tattoo of a bird with an arrow through it on his right forearm.

Officer: Do you remember anything else about him? Where he hangs out, his friends?

C: Well, I don't really want to give up people's names that don't want to be involved, but I know he has a pretty good drug problem so you could probably do a sweep of the usual areas.

Officer: Sir, I understand you want to keep your privacy, but the names of anyone he is attached to would be very help…

The phone clicked.

* * *

The bay was almost empty. All the tools and lifts had been packed up and the lounge was barren except for the broken orange couch that sat along the back wall and the table and chair in the middle of the room. T was determined to take the couch with them but C put a hard foot down. He had spent the last two days searching for a new headquarters. If G was found by the police, he could bet this place would be crawling with cops. He had found a good replacement in an industrial park twenty miles away, though it was smaller and didn't have a lounge like this one. He looked around the room, nostalgic and nervous. The others had been working tirelessly packing everything up and scrubbing the place down. The entire contents of their operation sat in boxes and plastic wrap in the corner of the bay. He had submitted the paperwork to the city for his personal company, C&C Mechanics, LLC, to relocate to the new building. They were to start transporting loads of equipment in a rented truck this afternoon and do a final sweep of DNA on the way out.

C watched the news incessantly. He waited patiently through weather and traffic updates for any mention of the police search of G. The story had caused quite a stir. Someone shooting up a robbery in progress was a good story. Someone shooting up a Cut Wrist Crew robbery was sensational. The news channels put out regular information with speculations and hypotheses on who it may be. The night after C reported his description of G, every news source was posting images and bullet-point lists of what to look out for. There was a nationwide manhunt but as far as public media went, nothing had been found.

"C." Doc had been wiping down the crossbeams of the drop ceiling though C had barely noticed him working in the same room.

"Yeah, what's up," he said without looking away from the computer.

"You have to see this."

C looked up from his work and saw Doc on an A-frame ladder in the far right corner of the room. He was holding the end of a small black wire that snaked out from the middle of the drop ceiling tile.

"What is that?"

"I don't know, it was poking out of one of the black specks on the ceiling tile."

"Hey T!" C called to the bay where T and Will had been organizing boxes by transport preference.

"Yeah?"

"Come here and look at this."

T came swaying into the room. He had bags under his

eyes and his skin looked pale. He had taken control of the packing while C looked for the new place. Over the past two days, he had taken only one twenty-minute power nap in the back of the van.

"Is this ours?" Doc held up the end of the wire. T furrowed his eyebrows and brought his head back, confused.

"No. I mean, I didn't put it there. Unless it's part of the unit. Where was it?"

"It was sticking out of this tile in the little black spec. I would have never seen it but when I was cleaning the bar I pushed up on the tile a little and it stuck out more."

"Hop down there, sport." T waved at Doc to get off the ladder. He grabbed the edge of the frame and took a deep breath. Climbing these six steps was going to take more effort than he wanted it to. At the top of the ladder, he inspected the wire. There was a tiny cap at the end, smaller than a grain of rice with a hexagonal mesh on it. T's eyes widened.

"Doc, grab me a flashlight." Doc dipped from the room and returned in an instant with a mechanic work light. T pushed the tile up into the ceiling and moved to the top step. Doc reached out instinctively and grabbed his ankle and the side of the ladder. As T brought the light up, he followed the wire trailing along the edge of the cross beam to the far edge where the drywall met the actual ceiling. There in the corner was a small flickering light. As the flashlight found the wall, T saw a small black box with an antenna poking out of the top.

"Uhhh." T stuttered, the light on the box lit up and turned off to his voice. T lowered down the ladder. He motioned to C and Doc to follow him holding a finger to his lips. They walked out through the bay door, grabbing

Will as they passed. When outside in the parking lot, they stopped.

"There's a microphone in the ceiling." T spoke quietly. He was pretty sure he was out of range of anything else in the building, but he wasn't sure.

"What!?" C's eyes lit up. "Who the fuck…" He trailed off. "Oh, that paranoid little FUCK." His voice rose as he spoke and he clenched his fists in front of him. "So that's it. That's how he knew. He had a fucking mole in the room and we had no idea. Fuck… Fuck. Fuck. Fuck." He put his hand to the bridge of his nose and rubbed.

"That's probably why the phone always echoed in the building. Some of those transporters mess up phone signals." T pulled out his cellphone and turned off the service. "Never know." The others did the same.

"Goddammit." C took a few steps from the group and stared at the ground. He recalibrated his thoughts, his eyes darted across the broken asphalt. His brain spun with gears and cogs. C could smell it burning from friction. Idea, no. Idea, no. Idea, no. Idea, no. What was there to do? The three men stood in a circle and watched him motionless. T started to speak but quickly realized he didn't have anything to say.

"Alright, fuck it." C spun around on his heel. "The cops haven't done shit. T, you come with me, we are going to do a sweep of the city. I think I know a couple places." He pointed at Doc and Will. "You two start loading the rental and taking things to the new place. The address is on the table." He looked them both in the eye intently. "Do not talk. Do not whisper. Get the address and put it in your pocket. If he has audio he might have cameras too. Go now."

Doc and Will scurried off back to the bay.

"Where are we going?"

"I'm not sure yet."

21 | ...

C's car spun the steering wheel to the right as it backed into a parallel spot along the road. The light from the Garage spilled onto the sidewalk. It was late afternoon though it seemed darker with the clouds overhead. The street bustled lightly as the Friday night crowd started to take to the strip. A punky couple with matching earrings stepped out from the antique shop on the corner. One held a few small items though their identity was difficult to make out as the shapes blended into the mess of colors and lines that adorned the arms that held them. The clothing store next to the bar was empty and the owner sat behind the desk dressed like a mannequin, looking busy on her computer, though she was most likely absently scrolling through the internet trying to figure out why her two hundred dollar linen vests were not more popular. A group of three girls too young to have their own money looked in the window at the clothing displays and dreamed of a future where they could strut down the street in flowing pants and large hats. The store owner looked up at the movement in front of her window with excitement, noticed the girls' age, and let her eyes fall back to the screen in hopelessness.

C and T walked into the bar and did a quick scan. They had been driving around town for almost three hours looking for G. The local drug spots, the abandoned train station on the edge of town, the strip of dive bars out east of 38th Street in the less favorable part of town. They even hit the alleyway behind the cinema where the theater had placed broken chairs with hopes to be repaired or picked up by the trash bots, but instead sat collecting rain and mildew and had made the area quite comfortable for anyone looking for a nice seat to smoke some crack.

G was nowhere to be found. Neither knew where he lived or even if he was city-based. They did slow drive-bys of the local convenience stores, peering through the windows hoping for a whole lot of luck. They popped in and out of bars causing some confused looks from the employees. They even asked a few of the local homeless if they had seen a man with an eyebrow scar and a propensity to shoot people. There was nothing. At this point they assumed he was most likely holed up in his apartment somewhere, pacing the floor, both proud that he got one over on the Crew and terrified of the repercussions. His image, or rather a poor mock-up based on bad security camera pictures of a mostly covered face and the extra information that C had given to the police, was plastered across the media. He would be boldly stupid to walk outside, but C was betting he was.

The two of them had come to the Garage in hopes he might have stumbled in but mostly because they needed a drink and a minute to decompress. G had been to the bar occasionally but it was far from his normal stomping ground. The Garage was mostly empty as it was still early and the real crowd would not come for another couple of hours. Two older men sat at the end of the bar, and a young couple made googly eyes at each other at a booth near the door. C and T sat in their usual spots and simultaneously dropped their heads into their hands, rubbing at their foreheads. Bob had noticed them walk in, but was in the midst of trying to leave a conversation that he was roped into about a movie he had not seen but was now hearing the entire plot described in excruciating detail. He pardoned himself with the excuse to help the new customers who had just walked in, and the people who had kept him from his job seemed displeased. Bob dropped two glasses on the table in front of C and T, the loud thud startling them.

"Good evening, boys."

C rolled his eyes upward with disdain.

"What can I get for you tonight?"

"Sour," said C.

"Stormy," said T.

"Comin' right up," said Bob.

This was a night requiring a little more than what beer had to offer.

"Where next?" T looked around at the other members of the bar as he spoke.

"I don't know. Like I said earlier, he's probably pinned up at home, waiting for everything to blow over." C stared at himself in the mirror behind the bar. He had aged today.

"He's gotta leave at some point. Knowing him, he's run out of his supply by now and is out looking for more."

"I know, but for all we know he lives thirty miles away and does all his dealings somewhere else."

"I don't think so. That transmitter was short range, a couple miles at most. If he was monitoring us from his home then he lives in the city."

Bob slid the drinks in front of them. T, leaned over the

bar on his elbows, grabbed at the straw with his tongue and took a sip. His eyes opened with the burn.

"Damn, that's strong." T let out a light cough.

"You boys looked like you needed a little extra." Bob smiled and walked away, reluctantly rejoining the conversation that had imprisoned him before but hoping his attention would be worth the tip.

C stirred at his drink. Across the bar, the door swung open. The man in the doorway seemed to be walking under a higher gravitational pull. His legs buckled as he stepped, his head swayed as he scanned the room. There was a crust of blood around his nose and his eyes were black. He reached behind his back, lifting his shirt.

"Fuck."

From behind his back, G pulled out a 9mm, pointed it at C and fired.

C grabbed the leg of his bar stool and pulled it out from underneath himself as he stood. In one motion he whipped the barstool at G still standing in the doorway and dove over the bar. T jumped backward, flipped a table out of his way, and dove into a booth. The bar patrons screamed and took cover where they could, the echo of the gunshot bounced around the space, seeming to never quite leave.

C was tucked under the bar, his chest expanding to its limit as he breathed quickly. He did a quick inventory of his body, there was no blood, no pain aside from his arms where he caught himself falling over the bar. He lifted his shirt and patted his back, he was not hit. In G's drugged rage, his aim was anything but accurate.

"You fff-ucker!" G fumbled his way over the bar. "You wanna kick meout, and then pu me onthenews?" His words were slurred and his voice growled. "Let's fuggin go then." He dropped his hands on the bar and tried to peer over. As he leaned, there was a slight movement out of the corner of his eye, he whipped around to see the black hole of a shiny barrel in front of the eyes of a young-looking kid.

"Can I help you with something?" Will was still-faced but determined. He didn't flinch, didn't move. If he was terrified, he didn't show it.

G slowly raised his hands from the bar, leaving his pistol laying on a coaster. He moved his head backward, trying to keep his face as far away from the gun as he could, and let out a light chuckle. In the most agile movement he could muster in his state, he swung his right hand and smacked Will's gun across his body to the left, ducking his head and body to the right and out of the way. Of course, his reflexes were not nearly what he thought they were. Will pulled the trigger on instinct and a bullet tore through G's left shoulder. He let out a breathy grunt, pushed to the right of Will, and kicked a foot backward, knocking out Will's knee and dropping him to the ground. The door slammed open as he barreled through it, hand squeezing his injured shoulder. C peeked up from behind the bar.

"We have to go after him." He grabbed G's pistol from the coaster and sprung himself over the bar. Will was still on the ground holding his knee. He was breathing heavily, fighting through the pain. G had kicked the outside of it and it had bent inward.

"You good kid?" C turned around as he ran to the door. Will let out a held breath. "Yeah, go ahead."

T slid out from behind the booth and followed C to

the door. Outside, a crowd of people stood staring from across the street. The gunshot had drawn in wary attention and sirens could be heard whistling in the distance. C scanned the sidewalk. In the distance, he saw a silhouette with an arm grasping a shoulder stumble around the corner into an alleyway two blocks down. The two of them sprinted down the street. The crowd of people dove out of the way screaming as a man carrying a gun sprinted by. One brave man tried to save the day by jumping out and tackling C. Fortunately, the same boldness, or drunkenness, that had given the man the courage to attack a person who presumably just shot someone, and was now chasing him down to finish the job, also inebriated his timing. The man threw his body weight a little slower than expected, got one hand around the crook of C's neck, and another around the back of his waist, but mostly ended up getting himself dragged. C did a quick clockwise spin without breaking stride, shrugging the would-be hero off, and looked back to see his arms lose the race to catch his face from hitting the concrete.

They stopped at the edge of the alleyway and continued at a steady, cautious walk. C had the gun drawn, pointing it quickly around the dumpsters and stacks of boxes that lined the buildings. T followed closely behind, scanning the fire escapes and peaking over his shoulder at intervals. If there were lights in the alley, the bulbs were dead. The center lane had a faint glow that spilled in from the streets but the crevasses between the trash piles were pitch black. C opened his eyes wider, trying to let in as much extra light as possible. The sirens had closed in and he could hear them a couple of blocks away near the bar. He was sure someone would direct the police to where the crazy man with the gun went and he picked up his pace.

"Fuck," C whispered. "We gotta move faster." They gave up the search and started hustling down to the end of the strip.

A blood-curdling scream echoed from behind C. He whipped around gun pointed, trigger fingered. T was looking back at him. Eyes wide, the whites glowing in the dark. His brows were furrowed and his jaw hung open. There was almost a look of confusion that alternated to concern. His arms were wrapped around his back and his knees quivered. Standing behind him was G. Smiling, eyes wild, red-streaked across his forehead where he had tried to wipe off sweat with a bloody hand. It dripped down his face and the glistening of the wetness caught the light leaving his face shadowed. One arm wrapped like a snake around T's neck, the other hidden, tucked up between the two of them. He jerked his hidden hand and T let out a desperate moan, squeezing his eyes shut. The pain was overwhelming. G let him slip out of his grip and watched him fall to the floor. A blood-covered knife remained clenched in his hand.

"What..." C was a deer in the headlights. He glanced at the ground and saw T, Sam, lying sideways on the ground trying to writhe in pain, but losing the energy to do so. A pool of blood was forming on his back, creeping out like the front line of an army in every direction. G lunged forward with his knife but time stopped. C's head raced, every sense seemed to go into overdrive, he could hear his heart pumping and the screeching of the sirens in the distance, feel the textured grip of the pistol, smell the sweat on his body and the iron from Sam's blood, see the fear in G's eyes. He flinched and started to pull the trigger but in this heightened awareness, he stopped. He saw the future unfolding, the consequences of his actions. Pull the trigger, gun goes off, cops hear the shot, fall in on the area, no escape.

The knife was closing in on his chest. C spun out to the left and grabbed the outstretched wrist. He slammed down the butt of the gun on G's hand. The knife fell. He let the forward momentum carry G, directing him with his restrained wrist, he lifted the pistol again and whipped it across G's face. C turned the safety on and stood his ground. G reached up to cover his face and tripped over Sam's legs, hitting the ground hard. Sam stirred slightly, groaning, panting. Curses and slurs filled the air as the two bodies on the ground untangled their legs. G made it to all fours; blood dripped from his face, his nose crooked and slick. A small pile of chipped teeth sprinkled the red puddle on the ground. He let out a noise somewhere between a grunt and laugh when a foot collided with his ribs sending him flipping and landing up against a dumpster. C was relentless. Within seconds he had knelt over him. Left fist, pistol, left fist, pistol, left fist, pistol, pistol, pistol. G's grunting stopped. There was no screaming, no gunfire, no ethereal soundtrack. It was quiet in between the buildings. Only the sound of clinking metal and the subtle breaking of bones. A split second of weightlessness took over. C looked down on himself from ten feet above and his head spun lightly. The crackle of police radios down the street brought him back. He turned to Sam.

"Sam," he called in a loud whisper. There was no answer. He looked at the entrance to the alleyway. Shadows from the street lights danced. He lifted himself and stumbled back. There was no more stirring. "Sam, come on, we gotta go." He grabbed Sam by the armpit and rolled him on his back. The panting had stopped. Nothing happened. C reached up and put his fingers to Sam's neck.

* * *

The cops peered around the corner, guns drawn, and filed in one by one taking cover behind the dumpsters. In the distance, they saw two masses on the ground. They approached carefully, the two in the front swept the shadows, calling their clears and moving in coordinated choreography. Two more crept behind them, one watching the bodies, one with eyes on the far opening of the alley. The last one walked backward, gun fixed on the sidewalk where they entered. In the distance, a police officer walked a line of caution tape between cones. While the rest of the team continued to clear the space, the middle two circled the bodies and looked for signs of life. One looked as if he had been hit in the face by a truck, a bullet hole through his left shoulder leaked, eyes swollen shut, skull dented in on the right side. The other looked untouched but lay in a small red puddle that continued to roll out on the asphalt.

22 | RECUPERATING

Five blocks down, C ducked into an alcove between buildings. The space was only a few feet bigger than the dumpster that sat in it but there was space enough behind it for what looked like the remnants of a homeless person's bed. Cardboard lined the ground and bent up in a U along the edges. Half a sleeping bag lay crumpled at the top right corner and various empty packs of cigarettes lay among the trash. An empty bottle of Jack Daniels stood in the center of the mat, a light film of brown liquid coated the bottom. A dim yellow light in a fogged plastic cover flickered above as a small party of insects beat at it aggressively, their shadows giving life to the ground. On the street, a sparse parade wandered along the sidewalk away from the direction of The Garage as the police pushed their perimeter. Conversations that included phrases like "active shooter" and "mad man with a gun" and "murdered two people" bounced around the walls. C kept an ear out.

To the right of the dumpster, under a gutter drain, was a pool of what he hoped to only be water. The puddle rested in a pothole that was deeper than he thought, and as he submerged his hands to wash, there was a soothing shock of coolness. He had flipped his shirt inside out as he left the alley to try and cover the blood splatters but some of the bigger stains were now starting to seep through. Carefully, he removed his shirt trying to avoid dragging any more blood across his face. The gun he had was tucked tightly in the back of his waistband and now the grip stuck out. He made sure to keep his back to a wall. The sounds of sirens still echoed in the distance, getting closer. He dropped the shirt in the puddle and used it as a rag to clean off his body. The outcropping was small enough that he could reach the water while being somewhat concealed behind the dumpster. A patrol car rolled past with its lights on but no siren. The reflection of the strobe bounced off the water and C fell backward out of sight of the road, waiting a beat before leaning forward again. He finished rinsing off the best he could and checked his face with his phone. He looked like shit; like he belonged in the vagrant's bed he sat in.

His breath stuttered and his eyes swelled and glazed. In his head, everything was screaming, a file room on fire. As he lay back he tried to let the events of the night process from the beginning, staying away from the end. Before his head hit the cardboard, he heard a voice pass with more authority than the standard bar crawler. C sprung up and crouched behind the dumpster, staying tight to the metal wall, wary of the movement of his shadow.

"Tell him he will be allowed back once everything is secure." The radio clicked. A muffled voice returned. The radio let out a digital chime. "Well, send someone to me and I'll come back. I'm going to finish this block first." The voice got quieter and moved further away. C waited a few seconds and sat back down. He put his head back and placed it on the cardboard. The ceiling above him spun slowly, the ground felt like a ship on water. He wanted to slam his fist into the wall, into the dumpster, take the empty bottle of whiskey and smash it in the street, but he kept quiet, silently muttering to himself. He rubbed at his eyes, at his face, wondering how hard he had to rub before the skin came off. He curled to the side and stared out under the dumpster to the sidewalk and the street beyond, unable to get up and advance time. If the world continued moving, then the past was set in stone. His eyes clenched shut tight, as if the muscles could burst through, and he relaxed. Deep breaths, sliding fingers back and forth across the smoothly-ribbed cardboard.

Three loud bangs exploded through the air. The metal of the dumpster vibrated and rang with each. C tightened everything in his body and held his breath.

"Hey, guy, move it on out, we're closing the area." The dumpster was pushed to the left, clanking and skidding, unaware of its broken wheels. A head popped around the side. "Let's go. You can't be here." A radio sat on the man's shoulder and his badge glistened under the light. C stared at him, confused, unmoving. "Are you deaf? Get up, get your shit, and go." C stood quickly, suddenly very aware of what was happening and all of a sudden equally aware of the gun poking out of the back of his pants and his lack of shirt to cover it.

"Yes, sir. Sorry, sir." He did a desperate inventory of his surroundings but aside from the fast-food wrappers, there wasn't much. The sleeping bag. He quickly snatched the bag and wrapped it over his shoulders, he did another look around trying to fill the time it took him to figure out what to do. The cop stepped back and waited on the street. C made an obvious gesture to stretch and scratch his back, testing the position of the bag and his waist. It was too short. As it unfolded, he realized it had been cut lengthwise and was more of a strip of green polyester with some cotton hanging out than an actual blanket and the bottom edge only made it halfway down his back, leaving his waistband uncovered. He fumbled with the fabric, trying to look natural but coming off as spastic. The officer stared at him as he twisted and turned his arms, moving his blanket in circles around his body. C finally wrapped the strip around his stomach so that it hung over the top of his pants. He grabbed the bloody shirt and tucked it under the bag.

"Alright, let's go." The cop motioned down the street. C gave a small nod and walked out from behind the dumpster, shuffling down the sidewalk, clenching the edges of the sleeping bag together. He caught a reflection in a glossed sign holder and saw the cop walking away, moving on to bigger and better things than harassing the local homeless.

After a mile or so of walking, when he was pretty sure he was out of the search radius, C scheduled a car to pick him up. The driver was hesitant to let him in but after a lot of explaining and one lie after another, they were off. C stared at the passing lights. He hadn't noticed until he was in a more confined space, but the sleeping bag smelt like cigarettes and piss. He pushed the thought out of his head, pushed all thoughts out of his head, and slept.

* * *

"Sir, we are here."

C cracked his eyelids. A set of brown, unmoving eyes gazed back at him through the rearview mirror. The driver turned to face him and C's eyes shifted focus.

"Sir?"

"Yes, thank you." C gathered the sleeping bag around his waist again and the driver pressed a button next to the sunglass holder. C's door clicked and slowly swung open with a hydraulic whirring. The lights above faded on and C caught a view of his face in the mirror. He was amazed that the driver even let him near the car. His feet swung out and gripped the street. His arm swung up to catch the top of the door and he pulled himself up. "Thank you," he said again.

"Have a good night." The driver smiled and nodded.

The door closed itself behind him. As the car drove off, C glanced over his shoulder and saw the driver waving a bottle of air freshener around. In front of him stood the stairs to his apartment building. He was determined to remain stoic until tomorrow. For now, his only agenda was to get upstairs, take a shower, and go to sleep. He looked up and down the street. A couple walked hand in hand two blocks down, chatting away. The girl threw her head back laughing. They turned and crossed the street to disappear past the closed deli on the corner. Down the other way, a man held a door open at the convenience store for someone entering as he was leaving. He let the door go, unwrapped his new pack of cigarettes and lit one. C, feeling secure, dropped the sleeping bag and tossed it in the trash cans next to the stoop. He climbed the front stairs, one wobbly foot at a time, gripping the handrail as if the steps were covered in ice. The elevator ride was a dream quickly forgotten and the final staircase to his door was Everest.

He woke up in the shower as the heat opened his skin, the water rinsing the blood he had missed cleaning up behind the dumpster, and turning the runoff pink. Reality started pressing its way back but he fought it down, focusing solely on the water that hit his face, the steam that revived his lungs, the sound of the drops hitting the ground. Not yet. The shower handle squeaked as it was turned off. The smell of the sleeping bag was stuck in his nostrils. It made him twitch and blow out a hard stream of air through his nose, trying to void itself of the particles of ash and urine that clung to the hairs. Out of the shower, C dried off and took a few swigs of mouthwash to combat the bad taste in his mouth. He wrapped his robe around him and made it back to the bedroom.

Curled up between two pillows, his cat paid him no attention. She was tucked away in her own dreams, a faint smile on her face and a soft purr emanating from nowhere in particular. C laid down next to her for a brief second and pressed his nose into her fur. Her head popped up, assessed the situation, and returned to her position, purring slightly louder. What was intended to be a quick pit stop on the bed turned permanent. C's mind wandered from what he meant to do to everything else.

He let himself fall away into thought, into the darkness he had been fending off for the last two hours. His body trembled tightly, his eyes watered slightly, his breath shook lightly. Memories of Sam chopped through the constant replay of the night. Stalking down the alley, intercut with a vague night at a bar from seven or eight years ago. The sound of bashing bones, mixed with making eye contact through the crowd of a concert. The muscles contracting on Sam's face, mixed with him at their baby shower. The face was haunting. It stood like a billboard on the back of his eyelids, a watermark on every thought. C clenched his fists tight, trying to push his fingers through his palms. With even a drop more energy he could tear the room apart, and he would, but for now, the most he could muster was the sequential tensing of every muscle in his body, like an emotional dry heave. Before long, his fingers would not stretch, his legs would not stir, and his head would not strain. He slept.

23 | EL

(Two years ago)

The flowers on the table hung stiffly over the edge of the vase, their petals scattered across the table, a light breeze taking them elsewhere. There was water in the vase but the nutrients had run out and they had only been alive because they weren't fully dead. Now they were. The stems bent and split, the leaves crumbled and cracked, the petals withered and tore. Once the most beautiful thing the planet had to offer, they were now decrepit and smelt of decay.

Elizabeth walked in the door. She took off her long black coat and placed it on a hanger, her bag slung over a hook and her keys next to it, her shoes lined up along the floorboard. C slouched into the couch and chewed on a sandwich. El made her way into the kitchen, stepping over a strewn shirt and bag. The countertop was littered with crumbs and bits of lettuce. A mayonnaise-covered knife was splattered on the black granite as if there was a loose attempt to throw it in the sink.

"What is this?" There was no response. "Hey, this mess in here, you gonna clean it up?" Still nothing. She let out an abrasive sigh and walked to the couch. "Hey, I'm talking to you." C continued looking at the TV responsive-less. She rubbed her forehead with her fist and sat down on the couch. "Why are you doing this? Huh? You think you can just give up and let the world go on without you? You think you can waste away in here and magically things will get better? It's not gonna happen. If you want to give up you can do it somewhere else." C didn't move. She stood up in frustration but stopped herself and switched tactics for the hundredth time. She fell back down into the couch. "Can you please help me out here? I'm having a hard time too. I get it. Everything is really hard. You think this is easy for me? You think I just moved on? I didn't, babe. I'm struggling too. But the only way it's gonna get better is to keep going." She reached out and took his hand. This conversation could have been on a broken record somewhere.

Nothing.

The news cycled through its daily routine. A special came on about theft in the age of the PII. One man tried to cut someone's hand off and scan it on his computer. A second cut the device out entirely and tried to place it loosely in his own wrist. The anchors bounced back and forth in discussion, calling in an "expert" who assured them there were numerous safeguards in place that would make the PII useless outside the body. He said the men were wasting their time and doing nothing but seriously harming innocent people. The anchors pushed back with a story of a guy who held up a man at gunpoint and forced him to scan his PII at an ATM. The expert explained that would be no different from the same thing happening with a debit card transaction and their attempts to under-mine new technology just because they didn't understand it was foolish and pitiful.

El switched the channel. "These guys are dumb."

"Why?" It was the first thing C had said in a week. She was taken aback.

"People just doing dumb stuff to make money. If they even did the smallest amount of research before cutting someone's hand off they would give up."

"I think they are just trying to find the crack in the system." She squinted her eyes in curiosity. He hadn't participated in a conversation in almost a month.

"Well, they won't. They locked them down so aggressively just to prevent this. I saw another article about it." She realized she could keep it going. "How would you do it?"

C sat for a moment and said nothing. She had lost him… until he opened his mouth again. "I would create the human body outside the arm."

She played with the lump under her wrist, pushing it back and forth. It glowed orange softly. "Interesting." C took the last bite of his sandwich and laid out on the couch. El gave him room. They sat in silence for a second.

"You're right. They are dumb." C rubbed his eyes and adjusted his neck.

She looked at him, studied his eyes, his body. They sat in silence for a very long time. El finally dropped her head. "Honey, I know you are having a hard time. I'm trying to give you what I think you need in space or support, but you are not the only person who is struggling. This can't be one-sided. You're leaving me to do this whole thing alone." She reached a hand out to stroke his leg. "I need your help too."

"I need to go take care of some stuff." C swung his leg off the couch and left the room.

El dropped her head. Where was the line between understanding and frustration? She tried to reach out, to pull back, to send help. He had been a ghost since Charlie. There was counseling and hand-holding, fights and rage. She saw her husband in there, but he was so far away. There was something else too. A distraction. Another avenue he had taken without her and now his mind was only there. She stood from the couch and went back to the kitchen.

He spent his days away and his nights scrolling through his computer. It was secretive though. He kept the screen close and his hand hovered over the quit buttons. *Was it an affair? Gambling?* She went through the gamut of what he could be doing that was clearly more important than his life here, more important than helping her cope, more important than their loss. Once the crumbs were swept and the sink was wiped she laid down on the couch and placed her arms over her face.

How much longer? She couldn't handle more. It was one thing to be removed, distraught, scared, but what he was doing now was cruel. Weeks and months of dragging along, coaxing every word, it was more than she wanted. She rolled to her side. *He's not the only victim. He doesn't deserve to leave like this. Leave me like this.* She had gone through her grief, her mourning. She had to be strong for herself, by herself, and now he weighed on her, pulling her back. It was unfair. She had to send a message.

* * *

C walked along the downtown strip. He avoided eye contact, tucked his hands in his jacket, and kept close to the wall. The people around him bustled on. They went to work, went to the store, went home. Their faces were blank and thoughtless. A man in a long beige trench coat dismounted a train and walked leisurely down the street. He carried a bag over his shoulder and his brown shoes creased as he stepped. There was nothing he worried about, nothing was weighing on his back. C could see the glow of his PII in his wrist as he walked past. The man had money. He could tell somehow. There was a way he carried himself, afraid of nothing, threatened by nothing, a victim of nothing. C saw no flaws, no hindrance. It was as if the man in the coat hovered above him at a higher level of being, free from the constraints of pain and disaster. If his shoes didn't crease you could believe he was floating.

The rich didn't used to be bad people, just out of touch. The best of them will still put their hand in a bucket of shit if needed, they just wash it off with nicer soap. They usually came from little and worked their way to the top. Their money was not theirs, they just owned it. Anyone could be rich, they just have to want it more than anything else. More than friends, more than family, more than a good night's sleep and a sit-down breakfast. People who hated the rich just didn't understand them. Now, things had changed. With so much government intervention the rich had become hoarders and hiders. People thought there was corruption before, never knowing it would get so much worse.

C scanned the road. Saw the Bots cleaning the street and sidewalk, brushing trash and debris into a small hole as their base, and sucking the cups and gum wrappers up into a large barrel behind them. Their solar panels glistened, blinding anyone at the wrong angle. A nice old lady sat at a hot dog stand in front of the town butcher serving bratwursts, knockwursts, sausage, kielbasa, hot dogs, and anything else encased in intestines. She had been there forty years selling the family business one bun at a time, smiling in the pleasantries. Across the street, kids played in the park, chasing each other and climbing in and out of a gazebo. C watched them steadily. The man in the trench coat walked into the park. A lady on a bench stood up to his approach and placed her hands on his cheeks. They kissed and talked and smiled. A little girl ran into his legs, throwing her arms around them. He bent down to give her a proper hug and then they were off, walking through the park, under an invisible shield. No matter what happened to him or his family, he could buy his way out.

24 | Onward

The street hummed with the morning work crowd. Hot dog peddlers lifted the metal grates that covered their windows and wiped down the plexiglass that covered the menu. Umbrellas were lifted and wheel chocks were dropped. The early birds of the food cart world blew fans over jars of coffee grounds in hot water into the middle of the sidewalk to let the drink sell itself. All they needed was the hesitation of some poor tired soul and they had the money. There was an early morning heat that echoed from the dew on the asphalt and the mirrored windows on the buildings. Clouds of steam trickled out and then exploded from manhole covers as subways clanked and screeched below the street. It was a wonder that the surface could hold itself up with the amount of missing earth beneath it. This morning's crowd did not wear suits and ties. They carried no briefcases and sported no Bluetooth earpieces. Instead, they came clad in brown boots and large jeans, high-vis vests slung around the neck, a twenty-ounce energy drink in one hand. They sported branded collared shirts that sold phone numbers and addresses on the back between the shoulder blades. Some wore sweatshirts with large hoods and scoped out alleyways that would be their pharmacy for the day, and still others wore little clothing at all, scraps of t-shirts and holed jeans wrapped in shreds of blankets. The smell of the street was sweet with good food, bad food, trash, and industry. It sang.

C sat in his car staring up the street. This side of town was its own. There were two grocery stores on the left side a block apart from each other. Across from them was a long strip made up of a nightclub with boarded windows, a convenience store covered in cigarette ads, a bail bond office with a barred door front and missing a letter from the sign, two auto body shops, and a twenty-four-hour fast food restaurant. C scanned every face that went in and out of every store but turned up nothing. He had been tracking the humans east of 38th every hour for two days but Will was unfindable. The area was not huge. Gentrification had pushed the lower class all the way up to the river. If they moved one more block over, some people might fall over the edge. Zoning laws and enforcement had long been abandoned. There was a clean delineation where the original roof was and where low-budget, local construction companies had tacked on the remaining floors to accommodate the demand for low-income housing. At this point, the five main skyscrapers in the area were almost competing with the skyline of the rest of the city.

C had spent day after day on a different block just waiting and watching, looking for Will, or his mom, or anyone he might know, but to no avail. Twice he was convinced he had found him, but after confronting one, and following the other almost to his front door, he was wrong. Now he sat, sipping cautiously at his coffee that he had picked up from one of the local vendors (it was not nearly as good as it smelled but not as watery as one might suspect), and bouncing his eyes from face to face. As he lost focus on his mission, he found himself watching the people not just for what he wanted, but for what they offered up. They each revealed their story. Their walk, sounds, dress, all told him more than they might have intended.

This line of work was a habit to C as he often spent days staking out banks, trying to get a feel for their clientele and putting together the summary in his head. He was good at pinning the rich, they maybe had one or two skeletons tucked away, but these folks, here, on the other side of the city were harder to read. They had bones upon bones, and they spent so much time collecting them that they weren't to be hidden away, tossed behind the coat rack. They, instead, were stacked nicely, organized and dated, always one more empty spot on the shelf for another skull. Their skeletons were their pride, their currency.

A girl walked down the street in a swaggered strut, her braids pulled tight and long, trampolining off the back of her black sweatshirt whose front showed two skeleton hands, one forming a two-fingered gun, one holding a gold chain. Her white shoes seemed to glow as they contrasted against her dark skin. She was rich.

C took another sip, the radio announcer bumbled along. A man walked out of the grocery store cradling a brown paper bag in his arm, a green trucker hat pulled low on his head. He was tall and lanky and his profile looked very familiar. C sat up, shaking a drip of coffee onto his hands and hissing at the burn. He placed the cup in the center console but when he regained focus, the man was gone. He turned off the autopilot and pressed on the gas. The car clanked as it shifted into gear, the artificial hum wobbled, a feature they added to the electric cars that were so quiet that they led to a slew of parking lot auto-ped injuries.

Creeping down the road, he swept his head side to side, left to right trying to find a glimpse of the man that seemed to have disappeared. In the distance, what at first looked like one body separated into two, and the man's stride unmatched the person that had been walking alongside him at just the right angle that C couldn't see him. Now the man walked a little faster, not hurriedly, but faster. C locked his eyes on him, glancing only long enough on the road as to not run over one of the dozens of people waltzing back and forth through traffic with ill regard.

This snail-paced chase lasted six blocks and, finally, the man turned left down a side street. C sped up to the intersection and just as he looked around the corner, he caught the man turning a key in the door of an apartment building. Quickly he turned the corner and looked for a spot. Most of the sides of the road were lined with old cars, most were gas-powered, a handful were first or second-generation electric, now on their third or fourth owner. The street was thin and narrow, if two cars passed each other they would have to pull their mirrors in to make it by. He went two blocks up before finding a place he could park, somewhat illegally, between the edge of an intersection and a stop sign.

Finally, out of the car, he carefully sprinted back towards the building. The facade was rippled cement with a brick base. Along the door frame was gold trim that was heavily mottled with brown and green splotches. It was obvious that, at one point, this building was an achievement of architecture, but was now cracked and overgrown, property of the people who lived in it. C took a step back and checked his surroundings. No one paid him much attention. He started picking through his pockets looking for a key that he didn't have. If anyone was watching him, they would have noticed him looking a bit too long, but in passing he simply looked lost. Finally, someone walked up to the door from inside. C noticed the movement in his peripheral, pulled out his key ring, and held his house key to the lock as the woman inside pushed the door open. He looked up at her with feigned surprise and gave her a smile. She offered a quick nod as she passed and handed off the door.

The interior design reminisced the history of the building. Once a hotel/train station for the rich and well-traveled, it now consisted of an empty front desk which rotted away along the right side with what used to be room key slots tiled on the wall behind it. On the left wall stood two gold elevator doors with an intricate trim of railroad tracks around them. Sitting on top of the doors were two analog dials that tracked the floors, though one was missing the arrow and the other's hung sorrowfully, giving a desperate wiggle as the elevator rose and lowered. Above a dried-up fountain on the far wall, etched into the stone were the words "Welcome to The Breen" with the image of the front of a train embossed just below it.

Around a hundred and fifty years ago, this was the final stop on a train line that ended at the river—before the bridge was built and everything was redirected. The hotel was a one-stop-shop for the upper class to take a weekend trip to the city and not have to hassle with transport to the hotel. Bellhops would grab luggage right off the train and take it up to the room. Metal cut signs hung from the walls directing to the two tracks towards the back of the building and a multi-foot thick slab of metal and concrete separated the hotel rooms from the tracks to cut down on the noise. That being said, there was hardly ever much sleeping at The Breen as the festivities were always abundant and long. After the bridge was built, the hotel's revenue diminished quickly, and the tracks were covered to make more rooms but as the area around it descended into chaos, the building was sold and bought, and sold, and bought, and finally revamped into a budget apartment complex for the cracked and overgrown.

C scanned the lobby for clues. On the wall next to the desk was a grid of post office mailboxes. The faces were nameless, sporting only the room numbers. C inspected it further and found the lock that the mailman used to open the whole face had been broken off and with a light pull, the frame swung open revealing a grid of open slots filled with junk mail, newspapers, overdue bills, credit card offers, and local restaurant menus. Along the front bottom of each slot was a white label printed with the tenant's name that would normally be hidden by the outer door. Three rows down and all the way to the right was the name Magnolia Arzhen. C remembered her, Ed's patient wife, and Will's poor mother. On an older, pressed blue label inside the slot was the number 369.

C called the elevator. The doors shuttered a bit as they opened and the floor didn't quite line up. Inside was the stained splatters of thirty years of late-night parties and a plastic bag that in any other situation would look innocent. To the right of the elevator, he opened the door to the stairs and started climbing. Three floors up he emerged to a tiled hallway lined with a brown and green carpet runner. The charm of the place was not entirely lost and, if you focused, you could see it the way it was, like the beauty of a once twenty-two-year-old circus performer, now in her nineties, wrinkled and hunched; the eyes are the same and the smile never changes. Her grace persists.

The walls were carved from granite and brass light fixtures hung just out of reach. C crept down the hall, door after door, 46, 47. The sound of TVs babbled in the background, 53, 54. The musk sat heavy in the air, 59, 60. A dog barked and set off a quick symphony of others that lasted until they all realized that nothing was happening, 68, 69. From inside the door, he could hear people moving about and talking. He knocked. The door opened. Will's mouth opened, but nothing came out.

25 | HOME INTRUDER

"We need to talk." C scoped out the apartment behind Will. The first room was the living room. In the center was a green floral polyester couch with tight cushions. To the left was a sixty-inch TV that might look impressive if you didn't know about the steady decline in TV prices. Second hand, they sold for only a hundred dollars if you got a bad deal. Between the couch and the TV was a circular tan rug—that was most likely meant for outdoor use with a wicker patio set—sitting on top of a hardwood floor, possibly the original. Beyond the living room was the kitchen separated by a half wall that ran three-quarters of the way across the room complete with a window that looked brilliantly at a brick wall. Perspectively, from the doorway, you could throw a rock through the window and do some damage to the brick wall. If someone sneezed aggressively on entering, the people in the kitchen might catch a drop.

C looked closer. The couch was not floral. The swirls and splotches were stains. A spot on the rug betrayed its original, white color. The kitchen was not modern in its open cabinet display, the doors had been ripped off and the hinges remained. The half-wall did not have a decorative white trimmed counter, it was a piece of painted plywood nailed down and the ceiling maintained the rugged outline of where the half wall used to connect. A pile of laundry along the right wall extended behind the front door, and through the open crack at the hinges, C could see that it was actually at the foot of a bare mattress on the ground which held a crumpled blanket. The left wall had two doors, the further one was cracked to reveal a tiled bathroom and an exposed shower. Clothes hung from the rod instead of a curtain. The light that flooded the bathroom was distractingly yellow and the one in the living room was equally blue.

Three people sat on the stained couch: an older woman, maybe edging her late sixties though with the face of dried apricot, a young boy with a Band-Aid on his chin and a piece of medical tape and paper towel on his forehead, and lastly, a girl about Will's age with a pretty face and a round body, dressed in what looked to be Will's clothes. The two kids looked at C, the older lady continued watching the TV.

* * *

"Who is it?" A voice from the closed door on the left wall cut through the silence.

Will fumbled, "Uhh…a..a… friend." He pushed C back into the hallway, pulling the door closed. "I'll be right back!"

The voice muttered something inaudibly.

"Is this your place?" C followed the cues and backed up.

"How did you find me?"

"Why the fuck haven't you answered your phone?"

"I threw it out."

C took a deep breath and stepped back. He put his

hands on his hips and looked up the hallway. A man knocked on a door a hundred feet down and was let into an apartment that raised its volume when the door opened. "Why?" It was a blunt question. There was silence for a while.

"I can't come back. I'm done." Will shook his head lightly. His arms folded and his attention was pointed to the floor.

"That wasn't an option. I told you when you started this was a full commitment job. I explained the risks, I explained the consequences. Things happen and we adapt." His words were aggressive but soft.

"Did you catch that guy?" Will's mind fluttered away from C's tirade.

C looked at him blankly, suddenly aware that he wasn't paying attention. His muscles dropped. "Yeah, we did."

Will perked up just enough. "What happened? Did the cops get him?"

C let out a sigh. "T is dead."

Will dropped his folded arms and took a step back. The words seemed to physically push him. His mouth fell open again, his vision shifted, his chest stuttered as it drew in the sigh that C put out. The head rush almost took him off his feet.

"Oh my god. Oh fuck. What... what happened?" Will's head reeled with cut scenes of the events of that night, of laying on the ground cradling his knee and watching the two of them sprint from the bar. On the way out, T had looked back and mouthed out the words "thank you," giving him a thumbs up. That image sat in his mind for a while as the ventilation pushed air around them.

"It's a long story but G is dead too. We need to get to

the new office and recuperate. Figure out our next steps."

"I'm not going. I told you, I'm done. I'm sorry, C, but it's too risky. I have people that depend on me to be here." He took a step back, minutely aware that C might physically drag him out of the building, but there was no retaliation.

* * *

Once upon a time, C would have done it. Would have made empty threats and forced the hand, but now the fight was over. Everything had gone too far, the rabbit hole had come to an end. Elizabeth was right. He took a step back as well and looked hard at Will. There was a resemblance to his father. The shape of the face, the deep eyes that darted as his brain turned. C's mind wandered briefly, trying to unravel where Ed might be now, how his long-lost partner had disappeared, leaving this kid behind.

"Was that Maggie in the other room?"

Will snapped back. "Um, yeah. I guess you would know her, right?"

"Yeah, she's a good lady. She put up with us like a mother, I don't know how she stuck by Ed for so long." A beat. "Who else lives with you?" C's guard was dropping.

"Um… my mom's mom, my brother, and my cousin."

"All packed up in there?" C nodded to the door.

"We manage." Will retracted to the door. "I have to go. Tell Doc I'm sorry too." With that, he opened the door.

"Hey, Will." C stopped him.

Will paused for a second.

"Thank you. For the bar, I mean. You probably saved our lives."

Will nodded. "Right place, right time." He entered the room and closed the door behind him.

C stared at the wood paneling for a minute. His mind was blank, his eyes matched. It's difficult to know what to do when there's nothing left to do. On the walk back down the hall, his head started rushing. What to do, what to do. He stepped over a dead mouse that he hadn't noticed before, as he entered the stairwell. To continue would be impossible. Finding Will was divine intervention, and replacing Sam was out of the question. With just him and Doc left the whole operation sunk. They had run their course, moved fast, made their impact, and now it ended, not in glory, but in strife, as all great empires do. He had made a lot of money. It would have been enough then, but not now. Not anymore. You can shoot an apple off someone's head a thousand times but if the first time you were too low, it doesn't matter how good you are now.

C walked from the building and stopped. To his right, a man in scraps of clothes relieved himself in the corner of a stoop, the sound of water pooling mixed with the sirens and shouts. At the car, he turned around and looked back at the building. Perhaps in thirty years the area will gentrify and this building will be revamped and listed as a historical monument. The mold will be cleaned, dead mice picked up, light bulbs changed, the arrows above the elevator fixed. It was a beautiful building under the dirt and weeds, filled with potential energy. It just needed a little money and motivation. A little bump, a little push. C tightened his lips in a small smile, and hustled back to his car.

26 | NEW PLANS

Doc's car pulled up to the new HQ late in the day. This home base was also in an industrial compound, and was sandwiched by two metal fabrication shops. In the open garages of their neighbors, sparks lit up and the sound of American industry filled the air. Men shouted and saws screeched. Somehow they seemed to compete in volume as if that would draw more customers to their side of the street. One shop's scrap pile sat in the yard outside and almost reached the roof. Pipes and fence posts stuck out from the sheets and car bodies. The street was lined with the trailers of eighteen-wheelers tucked end to end and forgotten about. A half-block down was an empty lot that may have been a parking lot once upon a time, but the painted lines had given way to weather and gravel, and now only looked like a random array of white spots on the faded asphalt. In the middle, dark spirals of tire marks created a black hole from the array of pop-up, not-so-legal car shows that frequented the area.

The unit C had secured looked similar to the old one from the outside. A squat beige building, though this one had two garage doors out front and an entry door between them. Inside was one combined bay and the only office space was in the back left corner. It was small and the two desks that inhabited it were mounted to the ground leaving little to an interior decorator's imagination. Large windows lined the office wall that looked out into the garage. The bay was only big enough for the van and the cover. There would be no pool table, no pinball machine, no orange couch.

The van was parked in the cover on the right side of the bay and a large pile of wrapped boxes took up the left. C had been unpacking the essentials but due to the hasty exit from the old place, things were not as organized as they should have been and he spent a lot of time digging through boxes of tools to find the things he needed. In the office, he had laid out the surgical supplies, the Psych Locks, and the gun, but was now digging furiously for the cube with the transfer program on it. There was a knock at the door.

"Hey man." C sighed as he let Doc in.

"Hey." There was a long silence. He knew. The news had spread that the man responsible for the Guarded American shooting had been found dead along with another member of the Crew. They had pulled photos from driver's licenses, mug shots, passports and cross-referenced them with the blurry pictures and video they had of the team's prior endeavors. There were news stories and think pieces complete with interviews from all across the country. Investigators, ex-criminals, and local police all chimed in to vehemently tear apart or passively support them. They had even gotten one of their early victims to come on and discuss their experience. It was the headline of every news source that the famed Cut Wrist Crew had lost two of their four and that their parade was coming to an end. The media kept it professional but the people had taken to the streets in mourning. Fights raged on between the rich, content with the demise of the bastards who threatened them, and the poor who worshiped the Crew as heroes, Robin Hoods that offered a vicarious hopefulness. Merchandise spread, shirts, hats, stickers, posters, memes; the country was in a propaganda war.

The two men walked slowly to the office. Doc took some time to look around at the new space. C knew it seemed foreign and cold but it was function over fashion. C drifted in thought to their old building, but with that came memories of T. He gave a light shake of his head as if to throw the images from his brain and pressed on. He took a seat on the desk, gesturing Doc to the only chair that had made it out of the pile. The two of them sat for a while, staring at the ground.

"I'm sorry." Doc broke the silence but didn't look up. He wrung his hands and tried to think of more to say. The classic "I'm sorry" was an easy, coin-in-the-fountain response. It was supposed to be meaningful but after so many uses it becomes a reaction instead of a consolement. There were no real words to express the emotion but offering condolences was somehow supposed to be good enough. It wasn't.

"I know. Everything started moving really fast, and then came to a stop and sped up and slowed down." A beat. "Hard to keep up, you know?" C snapped out of his trance. "But we don't have time for that now. Things are speeding up again one more time." He looked at Doc intently, his eyes buzzing, determined.

Doc furrowed his brow and met his stare.

"One more."

"What?" Doc let out a light chuckle as he stood up. "You're crazy."

C didn't move, his eyes fixed.

"You're serious?" Doc returned the stare, visibly trying to read his mind, to call his bluff. "We can't… I mean there's… there's no way we can pull that off. Who's gonna run the computer?"

"I will. T set up the system to be as simple as possible to save time. It mostly runs itself. As long as there are no hiccups I know the steps."

"So we need to train up G to help with the surgery?"

"G's out."

Doc's face exploded. "What do you mean he's out?"

"I talked to him two days ago. He's still shaken up. He was there. The night that…"

"Oh shit." Doc hesitated. "So you're saying you want to try to run this whole thing with just the two of us? I'm sorry man but it's just not possible. Not in the time frame."

C took a second. He had run through the scenario in his head. It was a tight fit but with the exact right movements, they could do it. Besides, it was only one more job. They could expend all their resources. Get the money, leave the gear.

Doc broke his train of thought, "Besides, without T who's gonna cut the power?"

"We're not."

"So our time is going to get cut even shorter. I'm telling you, it's a suicide mission, it's not worth it." C walked out of the room. Doc followed. "We all made our money. It was a good run. One more isn't going to do anything but put us in jail." C continued to pull at stuff in the pile of unpacked equipment without response. "C, you don't need the money." Doc reached out and touched his arm. C spun around.

"It's not for me," he spat. He went back to digging.

"Besides, we need to tie up loose ends."

Doc took a step back and sat on a toolbox. He took a deep breath. "Tell me the plan and I'll think about it."

C stopped what he was doing and closed his eyes. He tightened his lips. "Okay." He spun around. "We need to move very quick since they will almost certainly hit the alarm as soon as we open the door. Same as always I will help you get the Psych Locks on. From there the rest of the surgery is on you." C started pacing as he spoke. "We are going to forgo the sedation and you aren't going to have an extra set of hands so just get the PII out as fast as you can. I'm going to get the computer set up. Since the power will still be on…" He noticed the silver logo on the front of T's bag through the fog of some plastic wrap and dug it out with a mutter of relief. "…we don't need to swap power over." He pulled the cube out of the bag and held it up. A wall hit him, instantly taking his breath away. The color in his face glitched. A moment passed as he lost his words. A deep breath and a realignment later, he continued. "The hardest part is going to be the PIN. You are going to have to get the PIN from the guy while I log into the computer, which means you are going to carry the gun."

"Um… Okay."

"We don't have time to play nice so off the bat I need you to go at this guy. Get the gun in his face from the start."

"O… Okay. I uhh. I haven't used a gun since…" He wore his hesitation on his face.

"I know I make a big deal about the gun. You will be okay. Just get in there and freak him out. As long as your finger stays off the trigger it will be fine." Doc nodded slowly.

"As soon as you get the PIN, start the cut, I will come

get the armband from you and fill the charger. This operation doesn't have to be the cleanest you've ever done. Make the cuts, pull the PII, cauterize. Don't worry about the tourniquet or the forceps, just get it done. When you're finished, get to the van and start it up. I will be along as soon as I can."

Doc stood up and walked along the wall. He folded his arms and processed. His eyes shifted, running the plan through his head. He turned back around. "Are you sure you can get the computer system running?"

"Yeah, ninety percent sure."

He was fifty percent sure. T had explicitly shown C all the details of the programs but that was over a year and a half ago when they first started. He tried to rack his brain for all the details but without looking at it, it was tough to visualize. Even harder, there wasn't a way to do a test run. Banks aren't usually supportive about letting people plug things into their computers and play with their systems to steal money. T had set everything to run pretty autonomously which was convenient. There were only three programs to run, one to pull the PIN in, the mini bank, and the transfer software, but linking it all to the bank's software was the unknown. He could plug everything into the laptop they had and familiarize himself with where the programs were and what they looked like but if there were any glitches or if the system the bank used wasn't compatible for whatever reason, that would be the end. T could re-program on the fly, C didn't have that luxury. "Don't worry about that side. I will take care of that."

"So am I driving too since I'm first out?"

"No, I'll take care of that, I know you haven't really practiced with the cover."

Doc let out a sigh of relief. "Alright." He sat back down. "We can try. We are splitting 50/50 right?"

"You got it." C smiled.

27 | IT BEGINS

(Two years ago)

A small coffin lowered slowly beneath the earth until it stopped gently with a thud. A wreath of flowers haloed over the center with loose roses scattered along the length from people paying respects. A worn blanket lay to the side of the plot covered by a small mound of old and new toys. A man in black gave a small nod. C walked to the blanket and grabbed the four corners, cradling the toys. Elizabeth wrapped her hand around his as they carefully lowered the sack onto the foot of the coffin. When they let go, the blanket opened and covered the bottom half of the box, spilling toys around the vault. C's face was hard. If there were tears, they were falling inside. It was hopelessness with a veil of anger. He was stiff in his movements, his eyes fixed on the grass or the task at hand, never a face, never the stone. They stepped back as the vault cover was lowered in and set in place. Elizabeth grabbed a small trowel of dirt. C followed her movements. They both scattered the soil over the grave, took a final breath, and walked away, to be followed and cared for by the guests around them. Sam redirected and organized. C fielded condolences and prayers with few words and less eye contact. The world existed around him but not in him.

* * *

C sat at the corner of the Garage. The bar was empty and Bob was taking care of Monday morning business in the small office in the back. C stared at the half-drunk beer in front of him and pushed at the top of the glass, tilting it, letting the bottom roll around on the coaster. A light classic rock song played quietly over the speaker. Bob had taken a phone call earlier and turned the music down but never turned it back up. Chairs were still mounted upside down on the back tables from when he was pulled away and forgot to continue sweeping. Now a vague guitar riff bounced in and out of audible range, the clash of drums accenting the silence. The sun glared through the windows in front and slid along the bar with a golden reflection that made the wood seem metallic and impossible. Time was immovable. The bar that lay before him was a picture, a painting of a scene from five hundred years ago. The gold from the sun and the warm wood were strokes of oil paint slapped on with a palette knife and blended lightly. He was in a gallery somewhere in another world standing eight inches from a six-foot by six-foot painting that, for a moment, he believed to be reality. Soon he would shuffle onto a bowl of fruit or a portrait of a rich man in rich clothes who was important for some reason or another and now whose picture is bought and sold by rich men in rich clothes. For now, if he stared straight ahead, he could pretend he was in that bar five hundred years ago. The men in the other paintings might walk through the door and ask for the house ale and sit down to discuss the portrait they were commissioning. He would be one of those men. Men with no troubles, no ailments other than who would paint their portrait. Money could do that.

A car horn brought him back, his head once again racing with the thoughts he had come there to think, the plans he had come there to devise, the plot he had come there to write. C could feel the heat on the back of his shirt burn lightly. The warmth contrasted with the deep cold that wrapped around the front of his face. There was a flicker of sunlight as a person walked past the window which was followed by the creak of the door opening. A chime rang distantly in the back. C sat unmoving waiting for Sam to come sit next to him.

"Hey, man." Sam took a seat at the bar. Bob appeared in the doorway at the end of the bar.

"Whatcha drinkin'?"

Sam pointed to C's drink. Bob pulled the tap and dropped the glass on a coaster.

"I'm takin' care of some paperwork but just call out if you need anything." He dropped a couple more empty glasses on the bar in front of them. "If you need something from the hose don't bother me. I'll be on the phone."

"Thanks, bud." Sam nodded as Bob disappeared to the back again. He sipped at his beer, the bubbles jumping into his nose. He let out a crisp breath like a cold soda on a summer day and called out, "You pour 'em good, Bob."

"Shut the fuck up, Sam," a voice sounded from the back.

Sam swung his stool around to face C. "What's the news."

C took a slow sip of beer. "I have a plan."

Sam leaned in and whispered like a cartoon with insider trading. "What kind of plan?"

C was less animated. "I don't know if it's possible but I think I could do it. I've done a good amount of research, we'd have to do more. A lot more. But I think it's doable. I mean on paper."

Sam sat back up. "Sounds exciting, what's the deal?" He took a swig from his glass.

"I think I can steal a PII."

Sam choked on a beer. "What?"

"Well, I know there are security specs but I think there is a way around it."

Sam leaned in for real this time. "Dude, what are you talking about?"

"I know it sounds crazy. But with the right team and the right system, it's possible." C took a beat and stared off at the ground behind the bar, running through the concepts again, convincing himself. "I know it is."

"I mean, that's insane. For starters, you'd have to get the thing out which would definitely kill the person." Sam stopped talking and looked to the back of the bar. "Can Bob hear us?"

"I don't think so."

Sam spoke quieter. "Second, you can't use it without the electrical signals from the PIN. And lastly, the thing would die and erase itself before you could use it anywhere."

"Okay, so you get a doctor to do a surgery and he can clamp off the vein or whatever. I haven't figured that part out yet. There would have to be a way to record the PIN electrically and then play it back to the PII on a computer. You could reprogram one of those gesture tracking armbands. There was a kid in the hospital that had a prosthetic being made by this company that we used to do business with. It records muscle movement. I think it would work. But anyway, this is the thing I've been researching, I had this idea for like a charger. The PII would sit in some of the guy's blood in a case and there would be an electrical pulse that would mimic the heart."

Sam's eyes bounced back and forth, thinking. He shrugged. "I guess. You'd have to do a lot of research on all the specs of the thing."

"We would."

"Oh no." Sam sat back in his chair. "If you want to go off cutting people's wrists open and get arrested for a whole bunch of nonsense, you can do that."

"Come on, Sam. I need you. Don't pretend like you wouldn't be gleaming if you found a way to bypass one of the most sought-after security systems in the world."

Sam stood up and paced around his chair. "Yes that would be cool, but everything would have to be so perfect and there are so many details like how to get the money out of the accounts and getting the PIN and the police. I mean this isn't the little equipment business you guys had at the Bot place."

"I have a plan. It's a loose plan but it's there. We need two more guys. A doctor of some sort and then a lookout. We choreograph it, right. Every step is planned out. When we hit a roadblock we figure out some system or technology around it. It just takes research."

Sam stared at him.

"It could be a lot of money, Sam."

"Ughhh. Alright, alright. I'll help you do the research." He threw a finger up. "I'm not in yet. But I'll see what we come up with."

"Good." C took a swing of beer. "It begins."

28 | ONE MORE TIME

Sitting in the van, staring at patrons entering and exiting the bank on the corner, C took mental notes. He took in every accessory, clothing item, and shoe that he saw. Peering through binoculars, he read brand logos out to Doc who typed away at the computer. C knew most of the things he was looking at, but for the last job it had to be perfect. He had spent the last two weeks getting pictures of the interior, drawing mockups of the layout, and scouring the internet for reviews of individual employees as well as the employee's reviews of the company. The Barron's Bank was for only the highest of society. To open an account required an initial deposit of two hundred and fifty thousand dollars. It was one of the last true money banks and specialized in people that had a lot of dealings in government transactions, domestic and foreign, where Angiocoin was not accepted. This was the bank.

Of course, being of the status it was, security was expected to be top-notch, and therefore deterred any horseplay, but C had found something else. Fifteen years ago someone had tried to rob the bank and, with the press of a button, the alarm went off, and the doors locked to keep the perpetrator in custody. What they didn't expect was that the guy with the gun would go on a rampage and shoot everyone in the building until someone opened the door. When they didn't, he dropped a homemade grenade at the entrance and blew the doors open, killing two police officers who were approaching. This news story was famous for about two weeks, an internet meme for three, and a passing memory in four. What wasn't broadcasted was a leaked employee manual with updated procedures on robberies. Instead of a total lockdown, "for the safety of our employees and patrons," the alarm was to be pressed and the robber was to be allowed to leave without interference. The bank, instead, replaced one of its security team members with a private investigator who, in the incident of a robbery, would personally follow the criminals until the police could intercept them. That was fuck-you money. Up until now, the bank was an impossible job for the Crew because the investigator would just follow them to their truck and blow their whole plan. This time was different.

A light sheen of sweat glared on C's forehead. The day was warm and his long sleeves were unforgiving. The engine stayed off to retain gas and therefore the air conditioning was a no-go. They had been sitting in the spot next to the bank for three hours when a woman walked down the sidewalk and up the front steps. C tracked her. Her shoes were made by an exclusive French designer that C had not seen before in person. She must have had ties with a fashion company as her bag was not yet released to the public. Around her neck was a necklace, made of, what C counted, at least six diamonds, though it was tough to see through the binoculars when the run reflected from them. Her whole outfit, minus the diamonds, was, at minimum, several thousand dollars depending on what kind of underwear she had on. And then he recognized her face.

"That's it." C put his binoculars in the center console and put his hat on. "You ready?"

Doc inhaled quickly and exhaled slowly. He gave a sharp nod and pulled his mask around his ear. He matched C's eyes. "Let's get it."

The van pulled up to be parallel with the front door of the bank. The two of them slid from their seats, bags in hand, and hustled up the front steps, the van honked behind them as C locked it. Doc shoved the wood panel in the bank's outer door lock and kicked the inner door.

"Everyone on the fucKING GROUND RIGHT NOW!" He started awkwardly but a wave of adrenaline hit him mid-sentence. The bank contained only one other patron besides the woman they were targeting. Two people stood behind the counter and the security guard stood next to the door. The second they entered, the button under the desk had been pushed, they were sure of it.

00:00

Doc pointed the gun at the security guard and pulled the guard's gun from the holster before he could reach it. He pocketed the guard's pistol and forced him to the ground. C whipped a Psych Lock around the woman's torso. The force of the contraction sent her to the ground. She kicked furiously. The people behind the counter had disappeared under the desk. The one other customer cowered in the corner, thanking every god under the sun that they had gone for the woman and not for him.

00:08

"Everyone out from the back, now!" Doc had eyes on the guard and the other patron. "Face to the wall, hands on your head." He tried to remember all the points that G had hit about crowd control but it wasn't innate. The two cashiers moved out from behind the desk. They were followed by a manager who should have stayed hidden in the back. He came out with the thought that he could negotiate, entered the room where a man was pointing a gun at him, and vomited quietly.

00:20

C slapped the second Psych Lock around the woman's legs and made a dash for the desk. Doc ran to the woman and dropped to his knees. He snagged the gesture tracker, strapped it to her arm, and placed the barrel of the gun to the side of her head.

"Give me your PIN." He stared her in the eyes, unmoving.

The woman C had selected was an independently wealthy real estate mogul who tendered deals with everyone from celebrities to Middle Eastern princes. Though many of her clients paid her in Angiocoin, dealing on the back end of property taxes and the federal regulation of land sales, she surely had a large amount of federal money available. She was once married to an abusive husband who leached money from her and, before her personal success, dabbled in commercial real estate where she took out her home frustrations on her boss who ended up being fired for claims of discrimination by her. This was all very public knowledge as a series of court cases and political scandals made their way to the headlines featuring her.

With all this, the woman on the ground currently resisting was clearly familiar with how to handle demanding men. She wasn't budging.

Doc recognized the determination in her eyes. "Ma'am, I don't have time for this right now. You're going to give me your PIN or I'll shoot you and move on to that guy." He gestured to the man in the fetal position in the corner.

Meanwhile, C had dragged one of the employees behind the desk and, with a hand on the back of his neck, forced him to log in to the computer. He plugged in the cube and the cord for the gesture tracker and stared at the applications in the folder.

00:30

Doc let out a sigh. He placed the gun to the left of the woman's head and pulled the trigger twice. Bullets flew into the tile on the ground letting out a muted bang. Even with the silencer, the woman was most likely now deaf in that ear. She screamed. The room screamed. C's head jerked up to assess the situation. He saw Doc with a gun pointed at the ground, but there was no blood splatter, and the woman's legs still writhed in their constriction. He went back to opening programs.

"Now we're gonna try again." Doc replaced the gun to her temple. The woman breathed heavily but still didn't budge. She had a fire in her eyes that mostly covered the pain but she was losing the battle. Doc rolled his eyes in frustration. He pushed the hot end of the silencer against the woman's arm. She tensed and grunted with the pain of burning metal.

"Fuck you." She spat at him.

00:38

Doc was moving from impatient to nervous. Normally they had the time to harass the target for a minute or so if this happened. Now, they were working in seconds. He started getting frantic. C had finished his setup and was waiting for the armband. He looked up at Doc who gave him a look of hesitation. Time was running out, he looked around and saw Sam's backpack. Light bulb. He jammed his hand in the bag, searching frantically. Nothing. He looked around the desk. No. He pulled open the top drawer on the right side. Bingo. Springing over the desk, he slid into position next to the woman's head.

"Listen here, lady." He licked his lips and held a pair of scissors in his fist, jamming them up to her neck. "We need that PIN right now." He breathed heavily in her ear and caressed her cheek with his other hand. The scissors pushed deeper, tenting the skin.

The woman went pale. Her resilience drained as the madman with the scissors threatened to cut her throat. Finally, she gestured out her PIN.

00:58

C grabbed the gesture tracker and sprinted back to the desk. Doc proceeded with the sloppiest surgery he had done since he joined the gang. With no drugs and no one to hold the arm, the woman swung her wrist back and forth defiantly. He was able to kneel on her hand but the flexing of the muscles made precision almost impossible. He stabbed at the wrist above the PII and made a jagged cut down the skin. The PII revealed itself. Grabbing the device with forceps, he ripped at it making quick slices on either side. The woman was screaming in pain as her blood spilled across the floor. As fast as he could, he grabbed the syringe, drew enough to half fill the charger, and dropped the PII in. The woman had only lost about a half-liter of blood but against the white marble tiled floor, it was a murder scene. The cauterization was awkward and messy but the wound was closed and the woman was alive.

At the computer, C had everything plugged in. The program to pull the PIN was a simple upload from the device and stored itself by default on the cube for future use. Luckily the bank was using a standard processing system and the transfer software integrated itself without issue. Thanks, Sam. C pulled up the woman's account and uploaded the PIN when asked for verification. Her balance sat in front of him in four accounts, most likely a checking, savings, investments, and emergency. The total stood out in larger numbers at the bottom. C's eyes shifted focus. 2.8 million dollars sat in this account alone. Generally, in past heists, the most they got out of a single account was somewhere around two or three hundred thousand. For the rest, Sam had to dig through their more complicated accounts, but here and now, this was for the taking. C let out a stuttered breath and initiated the transfer.

1:28

"GO!" C called across the bank. Doc scooped up the tool roll and ran for the door. Sirens could be heard in the distance. C watched the computer cycle through checks and loading screens. "Come on, come on, come on," he muttered to the computer.

1:34

People in the bank started to stir as they heard the

sound of relief in the form of wails and screeches as the police cars raced closer.

1:38

The computer dinged. With a smiling sigh of satisfaction, C reached for the USB plug. He hesitated. On the screen, he opened the files window and hit eject.

1:45

C bolted out the front door as the police rounded the corner. Doc was sitting in the passenger seat, with the window rolled down, banging on the side of the door in anxious excitement. The van was already started.

"GO, DRIVE!" C called as he bounded down the steps.

Doc looked at him with wide eyes.

"GO!"

Doc took a half second of fear-stricken immobilization, then slid across to the driver's seat and threw the van into gear. He started to pull away as C dove into the passenger side window. They were off.

29 | THE GET-AWAY

"Fuck man, I'm not good at driving this thing." Doc panicked subtly. The time for a smooth escape had gone. Police cruisers sped behind them as Doc bobbed and weaved down the road.

"You'll be fine." C grabbed the armrest and situated himself upright in the seat. "Make a left up here.

"Pull the vehicle over." A digital voice sounded from the officer directly behind them. The cop car was riding their bumper and everyone was fully aware of the mismatch between the power of the patrol car and the power of the van. Doc swung a hard left through a red light at the intersection, squeezing between two oncoming cars. The officer did the same. The police scanner on the dash updated their location and responses from every unit in the area put half the city's police force on their trail. Ahead of the van, another officer pulled out from a side street and parked his car sideways across the lane.

"Shit, shit." Doc spun the wheel and bounced up onto the curb. The van stuttered across the grass, narrowly missing a light post.

"God damn." C grabbed the handle above his head. They skidded back onto the road on the other side of the cop car. "Alright, we just have to beat them to the bridge. Try to dip through the alleyway up here."

"I don't know, they're kind of tight."

"You'll be fine. Couple scratches, no problem."

Doc pulled the wheel and the van tilted as it made the fast turn. He slowed down instinctually.

"Just go!"

Doc grunted and stepped on the gas. The van barreled down the alley taking out trash cans and scraping dumpsters. Out the other side, he spun back onto the road. The van took some damage which would have been an indicating factor that they would have normally avoided, but now was not the time. Immediately, once they were back on the main road, there were two patrol cars behind them, sirens screaming.

C looked back. "Son of a bitch." He rubbed his face. "This is going to be too close." A mile ahead they could see the top of the bridge that spanned the river into the suburbs.

"We can make it." Doc hit the gas harder. He bounced back and forth between the two lanes going to the bridge, occasionally skidding over the line into the oncoming lane and swerving back. As the bridge came more into view, C let out a breath.

"Fuck."

In front of the bridge, three cop cars had set up a roadblock to keep the van in the city and away from the highways. Doc maintained his speed, they were closing in. He looked to C. C looked back and nodded.

* * *

The police watched from behind their cars, shotguns and pistols at the ready. A row of road spikes stretched across the entrance of the bridge. The van came hurtling towards them. They exchanged looks and comments; the chief gave orders for each plan of action depending on which direction the van turned off or if it tried to bully through the barricade. In an instant, their plans became irrelevant.

The river was lined by a grassy park with a bike trail that ran the length of the city. It was generally bustling with people working out, strolling, eating. On weekends, there were mini parades that would sweep the trail and buskers took over benches, their music competing for dollar bills and internet hits. Under each bridge a permanent convenience store, deli, or cafe drew in the hipster crowd who sipped at lattes and ate croissants, watching the ferries go by. Every Thursday, the police shut down the right lane of the adjacent road and food trucks would line the park, selling fancy meat sandwiches and spicy burritos to the public who queued up along the sidewalk and then walked down the grassy hill to find a nice place to picnic. Children chased geese and geese bit children. Today, the people of the park carried on, until a two-and-a-half-ton white van came barreling over the sidewalk, down the hill, and launched through the chain railing where it flew almost thirty feet out before falling the story and a half down to the water. The crowd shrieked and fled to the scene. Police tried to get their bearings as all their planning went out the window. The van sank slowly, disappearing into the murky green river.

30 | AFTERMATH

"Yesterday, a white van sped over River Side Park and landed in the water near the 15th Street bridge. The event ended a police chase with what were believed to be the final two members of the Cut Wrist Crew. Just over a month ago, the bodies of two of the members had been found in an alleyway, where they had suffered fatal wounds from what appeared to be a fight. Police have recovered the vehicle but the bodies of the remaining members were not found. Law enforcement have been sweeping the banks of the river, and dive teams have been combing the bottom looking for any signs of the two men. So far, nothing has come up."

The image on the TV stuttered as the channel was changed. A police officer was answering questions outside of the precinct. He spoke quickly from a script that had been passed around the office for reporters.

"We pulled the van out of the river there and took it back to forensics who did a full sweep of it. We can confirm it was the van that belonged to the Cut Wrist Crew and it had a good amount of their resources and technology in it. It's fair to say it will be a while before they do any more damage to this city."

The reporter responded. "What can you tell us about the technology used to steal PII information in the van?"

"I am not at liberty to discuss the details but representatives from the company have been notified and will begin an investigation shortly."

"Has there been any concerns about..."

The officer interrupted. "I'm sorry. I can't answer any more questions." He backed away from the mic and entered the precinct.

The channels cycled through a handful of other networks. Sports highlights and daytime actors flickered through, unaware and unassociated with the current events outside their own pretend worlds. Their day-to-day troubles to reset at the end of the season. The TV landed again on a news station known for its left political leanings. A woman sat centered with images of the car chase scrolling behind her.

"A vigil will be held at eight o'clock tonight for the members of the Cut Wrist Crew just south of the 15th Street bridge along River Side Park. Candles will be handed out for a donation to The People's Organization, a non-profit that provides legal and financial help to low-income families." She turned to the right ahead of the camera edit, which caught her from another angle. "With us, we have a member of the PII development team to speak on the future of the device."

The TV flickered off.

"A vigil!? That's wild." Doc dropped the remote and grabbed another metal bar to move towards the front door. His tools soaked in a bucket of bleach. He called across the bay, "Hey, do you want something to eat?"

C pulled another bolt out of the car cover. "Yeah, I could use a bite." He set down the wrench on the edge of the table covered with sandy scuba masks and oxygen tanks.

Doc walked back to the car cover. The two outside walls had been removed and C was working on the driver's side door. Doc turned around. Behind him stood the mound of furniture and tools that still lay packed and wrapped on the left side of the bay. The top of the pinball machine stuck out lightless and dull. A poster roll full of band logos and thinly clad women leaned up against the stack. A box at the bottom had the word "Fragile" written across it in what he knew was T's handwriting. It would all be unpacked, but not now, not yet. He walked around the stack to the office where he grabbed his jacket off a chair. In the corner was a small trash can with light singe marks on the inside where clothes were burned and the ashes dumped.

"Let's take a break and head down the road. I think there's a pizza place somewhere a few blocks south."

"Cool." C wiped his hands.

Epilogue

The sun shined brightly, unaware of the happenings or mood of the world below it. We hope for it at a wedding and forgive its absence at a funeral, even expect it. But weeks later, after the casket is lowered and the dirt is replaced, it is odd to walk into a cemetery with birds singing and a gentle warm breeze hugging the skin. As if all plots should have a permanent fog about them that can foster the mood. When standing over a grave, it should feel impossible that people in a nearby park are having a picnic.

This cemetery stretched far and wide. Stones and pillars, tombs and statues peppered the landscape. Some marking the life of a person who lived and died taking as little as a bit of oxygen and leaving no more than a name on a rock. People who would be long forgotten, kept alive only as a hash on a family tree or a passer-by looking for their loved one and remembering that they too have a friend named "Johnson". Perhaps one in every million stones would represent a woman who invented a world-changing gadget or a man who wrote a life-changing story. The rest were drops in the ocean. Nice people who may have left a good feeling in someone's heart many years ago. Love is not forever, death is.

Will stood at the foot of the grave, staring at the small array of flowers and memorabilia. Despite the efforts of the authorities, the site had become a Mecca. For a month, people had visited and donated masks, candles, framed posters, and anything to be placed around a tombstone. It made the plots on either side look pathetic and depressing. Now, the traffic had died down and only the true fans stopped by to pay respects. This stone, like many of the other new ones, had a small scannable code engraved on the top right corner which, when scanned, sent the viewer to a video or a website or a music playlist. It made cemeteries feel wholly more personal. Being able to wander through and meet the people whose bodies had been left there made the dead feel less foreign. What had been a name on a rock was now a personal video of the deceased growing up, falling in love, saying goodbye.

Will scanned the code and watched as a young T juggled balls at a birthday party, left for college, hugged his sister. He saw him tinkering around in an old workshop, his mother harassing him for not coming to dinner when he was called. It concluded with a news segment. A lady sat in the middle of the screen.

"The Cut Wrist Crew lost two of its members last week, leading to what is assumed to be the end of the gang's reign. The public has controversially followed the four men responsible for the theft of an estimated one billion dollars over the past eighteen months. The group has stirred a mass of protests calling for financial reform, leading politicians to rethink their platforms. This morning we will take a deep dive into the Cut Wrist Crew's members and the inarguable effect it has had on the modern market." The speech was intercut with parades and vigils, followed by a clip of the funeral service. Will could see T's mom and sister, dressed in black. C standing to their side.

Will pocketed his phone and looked ahead at the grave.

"I'm glad his family threw in that news clip at the end." C appeared to the left of Will. "This thing became so much bigger than us. I'm glad he will be remembered for it."

"I never knew his name was Sam."

"Yeah, better that way."

"Why did you run another one? That was a suicide mission with only two people."

C took a second to answer. "Yeah, that was the point. Had to kill off the rest of us for the police."

Will let out a small snort. "You really think of everything." Will shook his head.

"Plus, I was always curious if that bailout plan would work."

The wind rustled some leaves behind them.

"You knew him, didn't you?" A beat. "Personally, I mean, before all this. I saw you standing with his family in the news clip."

"Yes." C kept his eyes on the tombstone, still wishing it was a ploy, a decoy, another joke that Sam had concocted to pull one over. "He was an old friend of mine." He took a breath. "He was the reason this whole thing was possible."

The two of them stared for a while in silence, unmoving. Finally, Will dropped his head and reached into his bag. C shifted his eyes. He walked around the plot and placed a small granite plaque at the foot of the tombstone. On the front was a sheet of metal with a quote cut into it.

"I'm gonna live forever, you can put it on the stone".
– T, The Cut Wrist Crew

The metal glistened in the sun. C's stoicism fell as he

broke into laughter. Will smiled. A tear crawled along his eye.

C choked back his laugh. "Did he say that to you?"

"Yeah, we were playing pool and it came out. Thought it was relevant."

"You know, when we started this whole thing I told him it might get dangerous, that we could get killed." C shook his head lightly. "He said the same thing then. Didn't miss a beat."

The two of them laughed again, shaking their heads, even after death, the best men can still make a joke. Their laughter died slowly and the moment stretched on.

"I wanted to say thank you." C turned to Will.

"No, thank you for the opportunity."

C gave him a long look in the eyes and tightened his lips. He reached in his pocket and handed him a small box. "This is for you."

Will furrowed his eyebrows and took the box. "What is it?"

"You can open it when I'm gone." C offered his hand. Will looked at it, rough and strong, the hand of a man who had accomplished something in life. He took it in his and shook it. They said nothing more, just a look of understanding from C, and of slight confusion from Will, a state they both knew well.

C released his hand. With a light nod and one more look at the stone, he walked off, pausing briefly at another headstone before moving on. Will stood for a minute watching the blue-eyed man stroll away to a future he could never guess. He looked down at the small box and turned it over in his hand. Inside was a USB wrapped in newspaper and a note:

"Thanks for running with the big dogs, I'm sure he's proud."
— C

At the bottom of the box was a scrap of paper with a phone number. Will recognized the handwriting.

* * *

(Two months later)

C flushed the toilet and washed his hands. He looked at himself in the mirror, collared shirt, combed hair, clean face. There was a sense of contentment that he could read in his own eyes. To him, it felt foreign, like he was staring at someone else. He scanned the rest of his face, assured he would be able to convince himself that he was in the wrong body, but he only saw his own nose, his own mouth. Though it had been hard, his old self was trickling back. The difficulty was giving in. There were moments when he caught himself slipping away, back to the grief and desperation, but he was getting better at refocusing. He walked out of the bathroom.

C walked slowly down the hall into the front room. She had done well without him and her house proved it. He followed the trail of framed pictures on the wall every so often catching a glimpse of Charlie's smiling face among the other relatives and friends. The last one he stopped at. It was the same picture as his desktop. He locked on his son's face and matched his smile. Though the years had passed, he could still taste the ice cream from their last night. Further down the hall, the front room opened up into a large foyer with a glass chandelier commanding attention. It was modern with gold trim.

"Charlie, dinner's ready!" Elizabeth called from the kitchen down the hall. C glanced towards the voice and looked back around the large domed room. He took a long breath, the smell of garlic and oil filled the air. He looked down at his wrist, at the small scar where his PII used to be. They needed to test the system, of course. His life flickered through his mind. Up until this point, he lived in the four minute bursts at the bank. Everything between them was slow and meaningless. In those four minutes he could forget all the pain he was in. He could feel like he was solving the problem. Now, time felt more consistent, more stable. He looked at the clock on the wall. The second hand ticked away, unaware and undisturbed by the world around it. No matter how fast or slow the world feels—the bad times that drag, the good times that fly—every second ticks the same.

GLOSSARY OF CREW TECH

The following is a glossary of the technology used by The Cut Wrist Crew in their heists. Some of these products and technologies exist today and are already in use in the world of financial security, identity protection, and medicine.

PII (Pronounced Pea)

The Personal Identification Implant is a tiny pill-shaped device that is implanted in the wrist. It carries all records of the owner including drivers license, insurance, passport, business records, criminal records, or any other document that the user wants quickly accessible. More importantly, the PII holds access to whichever financial accounts the owner chooses. Transactions take place with a certified PII reader and is unlocked via a Gesture PIN (some series of hand movements.)

The PII sits in the wall of the vein and is powered by a chemical reaction between the electrolytes in the blood. Along with the Gesture PIN, it comes with two bio-triggered safeguards. If the source of electricity is removed then the device shuts down and erases itself.

The device receives a steady signal of electrical current from the heart. If that signal is lost for more than fifteen second, the device locks itself. More than a minute and it shuts down and reformats, erasing all its data.

In order to get the information back on the device, the owner needs to go to a certified PII facility and have a backup downloaded. It is a long process of identity checks and affidavits.

To pull data from it, the user scans their wrist at a PII

terminal and performs their PIN. The terminals are specifically coded to only take the information that the company needs. That way, the local gas station can't get a hold of your social security number.

One of the company's selling points is the absence of GPS in the chip. It is untraceable.

The PII Charger

A one-of-a-kind device created by The Cut Wrist Crew. Designed to keep the PII "alive" for long enough to get the money off of it. It is a small black box with a clear reservoir on the top. On the front is a numerical display box, a power switch, and two arrows pointing up and down. The reservoir is filled with the target's blood and the PII is dropped in. At the bottom of the reservoir is a small electrode that emits an electrical signal to mimic a heart beat. The arrows on the face can adjust the rate which the beat fires. On the back of the device is a USB input that tells the computer the PII is being scanned.

Angiocoin

From the Greek root for blood vessels, Angiocoin is a crypto currency that has swept the nation. In an age where crypto's biggest struggle was its inconsistency in value, Angiocoin solved the problem by making each unit match the American Dollar one for one. The creators designed it to follow the gold standard as inflation rises and falls, making it, in theory, incredibly stable. It has all of the benefits of cash (untraceable and nontaxable) with all the convenience of electronic payment. It has become the default for all transactions from online shopping to buying a car to drug deals in an alleyway.

The Gesture Tracker

The Gesture Tracker is a black elastic armband with eight small trapezoidal blocks around the outside. It was designed as a new way to interface with computers by using the electrical signals in the forearm from hand movements, but the technology never really caught on. The company pivoted to use the software for prosthetics. The Crew was able to get a hold of the original design and reprogram it to record the electrical signal of a Gesture PIN and then play it back.

The Car Cover

From the outside it looks like a large box truck without wheels. The back door opens buy swinging out and up. Inside is nothing – no floor, no axles, no mechanics, all the way to the inside of the grill plate where the engine should be is empty. The walls of the cargo space is lined with black rubber bumpers and the ceiling has four large clamps that hang two in each row. When the Crew drives their van into the back of the cover, the clamps grab a hold of the van's modified roof rack and hydraulics extend out, pushing the whole truck shell up. At full height, the van's wheels sit in line with the truck's wheel wells and the windshields sit only an inch from each other. In this position, the whole vehicle looks like a box truck in passing.

Psych Locks

Five-feet long and one-foot wide with foam rubber along one side, these giant metal snap bracelets are used in the psychiatric wing of a hospital as a means of quick control. They are swung from one end and when the center comes in contact with someone, the ends snap like a spring and wrap around it. As the person struggles, the band tighten.

The Power Cube

A small 5x5x5 inch box that houses a battery and computer software. The computer at the bank and all other devices are plugged into it. It runs the programs needed for the money transfer as well provides an interface for the other devices (the charger and the gesture tracker) to talk to each other.

Acknowledgments

Thank you to the Captain of our Crew, my mother, Ann Marie, for her support in creating this book. Her exhaustive read-throughs and ideas have made this story better, and her design and publishing know-how have helped me launch my writing career. I'm very grateful for my editorial consultant, Oren, who gave me the first true understanding of the potential I had, and for Sandy, my wonderful proofreader. To my brother and sister, Calvin and Jill, thank you for letting me dump a whole ass book into your emails and for always giving me the encouragement to keep going. To my father, Jim, thank you for teaching me what integrity and a strong work ethic looks like. You are everyone's best man. Thanks to Joey for being my writing buddy. And finally to Stine, my beautiful wife, thank you for supporting me in all of my endeavors, through thick and thin, you have been the most amazing rock to keep me grounded. I love you.

"If you wou'd not be forgotten
As soon as you are dead and rotten,
Either write things worth reading,
or do things worth the writing."

– BENJAMIN FRANKLIN
POOR RICHARD'S ALMANAC

Author Bio

Jackson grew up in Hillsdale, a small town in suburban New Jersey. He earned a BFA in Filmmaking from Montclair State University, which was a dandy good way to expand his knowledge of story writing. In the middle of his junior year, he took a brief hiatus to live in the Panamanian jungle where he worked as an eco-tour guide and recreation director. After college, he moved to Denver, CO with a nice Norwegian girl. They quickly eloped, opened a successful art studio and bar, and then, managed to survive the pandemic as small business owners. While his wife ran the studio, Jackson explored several career paths including filmmaking, rigging, rock climbing, the U.S. Army, and emergency medicine, among others. The couple have since returned to New Jersey where they live with their rescue dog Putter, and their three-legged cat, Easel. Jackson works as a paramedic and is already dreaming up new ideas for his next book project.

THANK YOU!

If you've enjoyed reading The Captain of The Crew,
please consider leaving a review. Positive feedback is
both encouraging and helpful.

Visit Amazon, Kindle, Good Reads
or the book's website
www.CaptainoftheCrew.com

27198781R00151